A Season In Delhi

Published in the United States of America by
Rebel Satori Press
www.rebelsatoripress.com

Paperback ISBN: 978-1-60864-267-0
Ebook ISBN: 978-1-60864-268-7
Library of Congress Control Number: 2023946458

A Season In Delhi

a novella by

SCOTT ALEXANDER HESS

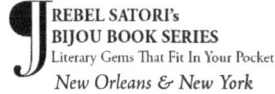

REBEL SATORI's
BIJOU BOOK SERIES
Literary Gems That Fit In Your Pocket
New Orleans & New York

Part 1

Chapter 1

They were perched at the wide-open mouth of Old Delhi facing the chaos of a blazing hot May morning. There was a visible haze engulfing the market and the air tasted of stirred-up dirt. Throngs of men, women, children, and animals, all burdened with strapped-on or shoulder-balancing loads, pushed roughly in opposing directions through the crammed streets as if guided by some divine order.

Brant and his husband Lloyd sat together in a bicycle rickshaw facing the crowd. Their driver Divit waved to the rickshaw behind them, where their house servant Hem Raj rode. Divit shouted something in Hindi then began to pedal straight into the throng. Divit was bone-thin, shirtless and ancient-looking with one missing eye. Brant feared he would collapse under the weight of them (his husband was a tall, thickly muscled man).

But the old driver pressed forward swiftly and with surprising vigor, bumping over the ragged, terrible stone street, cutting a path where there was none, barely missing a circle of arguing men, a barking dog and two shouting boys with giant boxes balanced on their heads. Swerving past the boys, Divit headed straight for an ox.

Brant tightly gripped one side of the rickshaw. He placed his other hand on his chest, guarding a precious ruby pin in the shape of a scarab that his mother had given him.

She had died just six months ago.

Lloyd shouted with hilarity. "My God this is marvelous!"

Divit turned the front wheel sharply barely missing the ox, passing beside the beast. Brant saw the giant thing's black eyes, its protruding ribs and scabs around its mighty snout and he choked on the ever-blowing dusty air, overwhelmed with a sense that he was breathing in something both magical and terrible.

He'd insisted that they see Old Delhi first thing, certain that such a vibrant onslaught of ancient life would obliterate any lingering fears he had about what had happened in the States before they left, that secret transgression he vowed to erase. He was certain Delhi would elevate him with its maddening wonders. But the hot air tasted of regret, of things stomped on, beaten and lost. He began to cough.

"Is that a cow?" Lloyd said. "It's so thin! This is amazing. You love it don't you?"

Brant smiled weakly, putting his hand on Lloyd's thick forearm as they pushed through an endless sway of haulers young and old.

As they turned toward a narrow alleyway, he noticed a tiny woman with a wretched little broom sweeping one spot over and over. Just over her head on a hanging wire, a monkey sat watching. Behind her was a crumbling building where men lounged on the windowsill smoking.

They came to an abrupt stop and before he could move Hem Raj was at the side of the rickshaw shouting for them to get out, motioning toward a corner stand ablaze with glittering hanging garlands and bushels of spices whose pungent scents nearly choked the air.

"Welcome to Delhi," Hem Raj said, bowing his head and offering a hand.

Chapter 2

If it hadn't been for the monkey god, Brant told himself later, he would have been safe, he would have remained faithful. But the little devil hypnotized him in a weak moment of lingering grief and hapless anger, seduced him with its ritual-like whispering.

The thing's exotic angular face, the broad feet and hands, an animal sitting on one knee like a man, yes exactly like a man, legs spread beckoning, demanding. It had pulled him under with a false promise of oblivion.

It began innocently two weeks before he and Lloyd set off for Delhi. Brant planned a solo jaunt to Cold Spring, to visit a shop his best friend Jasmine had told him about – *Charmed Antiquities & Curiosities*. Just an hour from Manhattan, it was a lazy train ride sweeping gently alongside a soft dark river past a rise of deeply green late spring forest.

Moving so fast and rhythmically along that endless river, dreamily picturing the landscape of his life with Lloyd, Brant could see it all stretching on and on led by his husband's relentless vigor and excitement. The car swayed, and as he dozed, he heard soft laughter slipping through that space between the sharp metal train wheels and the hot steel track. His mother whispered, "Look" and he glimpsed just ahead, wavering, an unrecognizable barely visible flatness, as if the thrilling landscape of Lloyd were fading too fast, or even worse, covering something dried and barren that he could not yet see and did not quite understand.

The train blew its hard, loud whistle and he sat up with a start. At the same time he heard a woman cough. He turned sharply, momentarily expecting his mother.

It was indeed an older woman with a shock of white hair. She was wearing a pink hat and a tailored jacket and skirt. His mother had maintained an impeccable fashion sense to the bitter end. Even in those final, unbearable bed-ridden days, she had insisted on earrings and lipstick. The woman behind him was alone. She began laughing at something she was reading in a weathered magazine.

The train slowed, the whistle blew once more. Out the window, the elegant river had disappeared, replaced with a graveled landscape fronting a narrow patch of grass with strangely barren trees. They looked as if they were rooted but dead in the spring earth.

He strained his neck, looking for the river behind him, and as he glimpsed it, he recalled a special trip with his mother. They were on a charming vintage train that ran along the Missouri River from St. Louis to Jefferson City. They had scones and coffee in china cups. She shared bright stories of her youth and then unexpectedly – regrets. "I spent so long propping up your father, helping him along to his success that when it finally came time for me I forgot what I wanted. So I took up tennis. Don't do that."

While the timbre of her voice faded and the touch of her hand became a memory, certain statements he held firmly in place.

The train inched to a halt. The white-haired woman in the pink hat stood up and hurried down the aisle. A porter shouted the name of the stop. He had reached his destination.

Chapter 3

He got off the train and hated what he saw. A bleached two-story tenement. A small café pressed too close to the rusty train tracks, wrecked little tables and a gray-haired waitress slouched and smoking.

The melancholic memory of that train trip with his mother lingered as he stepped out into the street. Their vintage locomotive had pulled up to a charming red-thatched roof depot decorated with shimmering gold and green holiday garland (it was near Christmas). There had been a light snow. She had lit a long brown cigarette (his father insisted they were meant for men). Then she had taken his hand. "I have a shop I want you to see." It was the day she'd bought him the ruby pin.

Brant crept forward, fighting a desire to turn away, to get the next train back to the city and rush to see Jasmine so he could share the odd, uneasy feelings he'd had on the train. His sudden doubts about the trip to India. Jasmine was his emotional rock and true soul-sister. In addition to being a talented performance-artist and gender illusionist, he was an astrologist whose readings and gifts of crystals had guided Brant through tough times. Lloyd did not share his husband's enthusiasm for astrology. He was an atheist and a pragmatist.

Brant eyed the terrible looking waitress who stared but did not smile. Behind him the track was empty. He knew the train ran on the hour. There wasn't even a bench to sit on.

This was the moment, he thought, when Lloyd would dart ahead and shake him out of it. He'd laugh that infectious laugh that Brant fell in love with. He'd walk too fast, talking all the while, his long muscular legs striding in a way that Brant could never keep up with. He'd make everything sunny. But none of that happened.

And for the second time that day, a hard sliver of doubt crept in regarding their trip to India. What if he stepped out and did not like what he saw – did not know what *he* was doing there? There would be no one to run to. He would only have Lloyd. Jasmine would be across the world. His mother was gone. The thoughts made him both sad and angry.

He took a deep breath, hushed his mental chatter, and strode up the street, toward a corner that cut sharply. At the turn, he saw the shop. *Antiques & Curiosities.*

It looked like a cottage, bricks painted rusty red, white shutters on two quaint windows, a glass front door and at the peak of the thatched, V-shaped roof the sign carrying its name, scrawled as if by a child on a piece of wood.

It was a fairy tale shop, dropped into this desolate town. He moved toward it slowly at first, then more quickly. He wanted to get inside, deep inside, because he knew it would be marvelous, safe and joyful, it would overwhelm him with its grandness, the way Delhi surely would, it would intoxicate and amuse him and make him feel worthwhile. This shop would revive his spirits. He would tell Lloyd all about it. He would buy a trinket for Jasmine.

The front door was strange. The frame was a very dark wood, and in its center was a rectangle of deeply muted almost warped looking glass. He could not see clearly through it and this sent a thrill through his body. Staring into the waved dizzying glass (like Delhi, surely like Delhi) were greens, reds, whites, swimming and blurred. He was entering a wonderland.

He pushed the heavy door open and stepped in. It was absolutely still and dimly lit. Every inch of the store was filled. Antique display tables, glass cabinets, bookcases on the walls, tall statues and pedestals, a very long counter. The counter was covered with striking and beautiful ornaments, nude ivory figurines hurtling forward on horses, clocks, small golden buckets of peacock plumes, shining, shimmering things.

Brant did not move.

"It's a bit much," a gentle voice said.

Brant looked over at the long glass case. He saw first, sitting on a large golden box and illuminated with a tiny spotlight, the creature that he would learn to be the monkey god, and past that, a tall, handsome, thick bodied man of about 40. The man immediately reminded him of a hulky film actor he'd long had a crush on. He also looked a bit like Lloyd, with his broad ruggedness.

Brant could not think of what to say, so he moved toward the man, who was smiling, and as he got closer, it was as if he were moving into a hidden cloud, an arresting rush of unfamiliar and intoxicating scents. Musk and something hard, spicy. It seemed to be coming directly from the monkey figure, pressing out of its thick paws and feet.

"The incense is patchouli." the man said, smiling. "We try to set a tone."

Brant stood against the counter staring at the ceramic monkey. The man, still smiling, leaning closer, lifted it up slowly and offered it to Brant.

"You like him," the man said. "Hanuman, a Hindu deity. The monkey god. Hold him. He won't bite."

He took the small but deceptively heavy animal into his hands and it was at that moment that Brant felt suddenly very unsteady. The smell of the incense was overpowering, almost sickly, the shop warm, and he felt as if he'd entered into something strange and dangerous. As if he were already a foreigner. He wished he'd taken the train back.

He gripped the figurine harder thinking it might steady him, bring him back to center. But the creature, with its big almond shaped eyes, wide sensual nose and open mouth pressing forward, taunted him and he swore he heard a whispering and it was at that moment that he felt very dizzy and thought he would faint. He slouched slightly forward onto the counter, setting the figurine onto the glass. He shut his eyes. The salesman put his hands over Brant's.

"Are you all right?" he said softly. "It's always too warm in here."

Brant kept his eyes shut and did not move. It was as if Hanuman were speaking. He liked the feeling of the big man's hands on his.

"I think I better sit down," Brant said.

Without a word the man guided him toward the back of the shop, behind a red curtain, to a small salon with a tasseled settee and a small table and cabinet. Brant sat as the man opened the cabinet.

"I have gin or whiskey. Or water from the tap?" he said.

The settee was a two-seater, covered with a dark silk fabric. It rose in the center oddly as if there were a bump there. Brant leaned onto one side of it, still dizzy.

"Gin," he said.

"I just need to get glasses," the man said with a quick odd laugh.

As he stepped back through the curtain, Brant noticed how tight the man's tweed pants were. He had a habit of turning to lusty thoughts when he felt anxious or afraid. It distracted him. Jasmine said he was likely a courtesan in a former life.

He took a deep breath. His equilibrium was returning. As he considered standing, the man returned. He stood directly in front of Brant in the small, tight space, holding two glasses. The tight tweed was equally revealing in front. Brant stared a moment too long.

"It's very dull here, I'm afraid. So few customers lately," the man said. "I probably shouldn't have a drink so early in the day."

The man smiled slyly, and waited, and Brant felt as if he were coming closer, pressing himself toward him. Then the man turned, poured, and came back to the settee, sitting on the other side of the odd little bump, handing Brant his drink. The seat was so small, they had to turn their bodies uncomfortably to see one another. Brant sipped the burning gin.

"Thank you. I feel foolish. I'll go," he said.

But as the big man lobbed his arm across the back of

the settee, his hand so close to Brant's face now, that hand smelling of the incense he must have held and placed into the burner, Brant did not resist a quickly rising and blinding desire, a blunt force that blotted out all landscapes, all sad memories and pulled him fully into a place of momentary abandon and bliss. The man sighed and let his fingers brush the side of Brant's cheek and that was all it took.

Later, at the depot waiting for the train, he soothed his guilt with a promise that this episode, this abandon that had left him half naked on the floor of a shop, pants around his ankles, spent, that this would never happen again. Everyone was allowed one terrible mistake, and this was his. He had been faithful to Lloyd since their marriage began and he would be faithful going forward. He would tell no one. This one transgression would die right here in Cold Spring. Far from India, buried and forever forgotten.

But that, of course, would prove impossible.

Chapter 4

Brant dug into the earth with a metal trowel. It was early morning and very hot. The work was slow going.

He wore a one-piece cotton white smock (a kurta, Hem Raj had told him) that hung past his thighs. It came with matching pants, but he hadn't bothered with them, so his knees sank into the grass. He'd bought the top at Khan market, which was not an actual market, more a cluster of small ancient looking specialty shops butted against one another in a semi-circle layout.

He and Lloyd had settled nicely into their 8-room ghost-white bungalow at the end of a whistle-clean street, a stark contrast to the grit of Old Delhi. Brant found the days very, very long. Lloyd left for work at 8AM and did not return until after 8PM for dinner.

They were nearing the end of their first week and Brant felt himself shrinking, losing any sense of purpose. His mother's warning when he announced his engagement haunted him *"Don't lose yourself."* Hem Raj had suggested gardening and Brant saw that as a sign. He needed a project.

Their home had a large back yard. Double glass doors opened from the living room onto the yard, where two wicker chairs and a wicker table sat. There was little growing and at first Brant wondered what he was meant to garden. Some twenty feet ahead he found a small bed of sad-looking marigolds, and a frail tree that tilted terribly as if it would fall over at any moment. The tree was black on the tips of its tulip-shaped leaves. He decided to stir up the earth around the tree, add some fertilizer and prop it up with new dirt.

As he dug with vigor, the earth finally began to give. He stabbed relentlessly, throwing dirt over his shoulder. He stopped, wiping sweat on his shirt sleeve, noticing several monkeys sitting on wires at the edge of the property. They were watching him. Mocking him, he decided. The ridiculous American outsider. He often felt like an extra piece of luggage or shiny thing his husband had brought along, nothing fully formed or recognizable to anyone in this land. Not even the monkeys.

"I see you," Brant said, squinting into the sun. "This is going to work. I'm going to create something."

There was a loud screeching, as one of the monkeys swiped at his partner. They both began crying and tugging at one another. He wondered what the fight was about. One of the monkeys shrieked long and loud, the other was silenced. At once, they both turned back to Brant. They seemed to expect a response.

He stabbed the earth harder and got back to work. He dug deeper. His plan was based on no experience, nothing solid but it didn't matter. It gave him a goal. He would rescue the sad little tree. It would bloom again and Lloyd would be awed by it all. His mother had kept a beautiful garden and he would develop this new talent to honor her, picking up where she left off.

As he loosened and tossed aside a particularly large chunk of mud, he hit something solid. He dug a little further and saw through a veil of dirt bright green. Not roots or anything of the earth. It looked like the spine of a book.

He dug faster, using both the trowel and his hands. He was sweating profusely, but he was certain he'd discovered a bit of treasure. It was a good omen, a glorious remnant from the past, drawing him right into his new time in Delhi.

The sun burned and he dug quickly seeing the back, the edges, the circumference. He pressed away more earth, then wrenched the thing free. It was sheathed in plastic, protected from the elements like some sacred text. He held it in his hands and it felt warm, pulsing with life.

The monkeys were quiet. He looked up to find them scratching themselves, clearly happy with his discovery. He laughed out loud at this archeological twist of fate. He may have found something truly important. The entire fabric of the day changed.

Hem Raj called from the patio.

"Best to stop," he called. "Heat."

Brant stood. His knees were aching. He pressed his discovery close to his heart then held it out peering through the plastic. He saw on the cover barely visible in faded letters - *Carol*.

He hurried in, giddy and a touch dizzy from the increasing heat of the day, but happy thinking suddenly of Lloyd, of a moment last summer, Lloyd waving and smiling in the distance calling "Come in for lunch. Come away from the lake." That had been a very happy day.

Chapter 5

May, 1945
This place is frightful.

The rest of the yellowed page of sturdy lined paper, was blank. As was the next. Then on page three Brant, who was sitting alone in bed in the soft glow of a bedside lamp (Lloyd had to work very late again) saw in a messy handwriting:

Miriam brought a bottle of dry gin and a shaker for martinis.

Scribbled in the margin in another color, a short grocery list: *olives, cheddar, saltines, hairspray.* Then below that:

Both Benny and my Gerald were off to the club again. Miriam said we'd have a wicked girl's night. I don't think Miriam has a wicked bone in her body.

She doesn't eat. Never. I can't crack her. I pulled out the chilled shrimp and that Turkish candy. Nothing. Her figure is better than mine. Gerald says he likes a girl with a few pounds but I wonder. He hasn't touched me in a year. I hate him for that. I blame it on his work, but who knows. I've stopped trying. My mother told me sex was the least important part of a happy marriage.

I'm really stuck here. Six months is a very long time and it's only been four weeks. Miriam isn't much but she's all I've got in this dreadful spot with a lot of bland people. Well, those like me. I should really get out and meet the Delhi locals. Mix and mingle, mother used to say, though that was the club, the fucking sewing circle. Not here. She'd never leave the house. She'd never've come here! People not like her terrify her.

But I will. I'll step out. Let Gerald have a fit. He really stopped paying attention to me long ago. The ass. Is this what being trapped feels like?

I've got to come up with a real fine scheme, something for us two girls to get into while our men skunk around at those clubs.

I'm barely 30 and feel old. I told Miriam that and she just set down her martini and pulled out her lipstick, as if someone was watching us. After taking her time fixing her mouth she said simply – "It will pass."

She's been in Delhi five months. It doesn't seem to bother her. The endless alone time. The heat, so much heat. "Don't do anything rash," Miriam said. I smiled, but decided right then and there I would do something rash. I'd buy something very expensive, or have an affair with an Indian man. I'd do something to stir up a scandal. I'd make a scene.

Anika is watching from the bedroom door. Sitting on this funny platform bed, writing in my pretty little journal like a princess. I'll have to go to sleep so she can leave me alone.

Anika is an odd bird. Cleans the house, cooks and spies on me. Always hovering. I am getting used to being taken care of I have to admit but I don't like her obvious disapproval. I'll have to turn off the light so she can leave me alone. Maybe my scandalous plan will hatch in my dream.

Chapter 6

Brant was sitting in a wicker chair in the back yard, Lloyd next to him. The night sky had folded into its own deep blackness - not star laden and eternal, more like a void disappearing. Brant felt he was looking up at nothing. He held Carol's journal in his lap. Gin martinis were close at hand on the small wicker table.

"What are you searching for?" Lloyd said.

Brant looked away from the sky, his husband was a stark silhouette in the darkened backyard, tanned and glistening slightly with sweat. He was wearing pale blue slacks and had loosened his tie and unbuttoned the first several buttons of his white shirt. A soft swirl of chest hair pressed through. His attractiveness was accentuated by a lack of definition, his form merging with the night shades.

"I thought I'd see stars?" Brant said.

Lloyd laughed loudly then stood up and stretched. His shirt came untucked as he reached his hands high over his head like he would yank some hidden stars from the heavens.

"It's Delhi, the haze is constant. We better start checking the air quality. It might be unhealthy to be sitting out."

Lloyd moved around to the back of Brant's chair.

"It's a very unhealthy place, my dear," he said, placing his hands on Brant's shoulders.

Brant pressed his cheek into his husband's hand.

"Then why are we here?" Brant said.

Lloyd began to massage Brant's shoulders.

"The great seduction is underway," Lloyd said. "The McGrath account will be secured any day now. We are wooing them and it will be my biggest win yet. You know what I say about face time with these clients."

Lloyd pressed deeply at a nasty knot in Brant's right shoulder and Brant shuddered with pleasure.

"What are you reading?" Lloyd said, noticing the journal in his lap.

"I found it," Brant said. "Right out there."

He lifted his arm pointing, disconnecting with Lloyd's touch on his shoulder. He was becoming aroused and knew Hem Raj was still in the house. He didn't want to make the wrong impression so early. Also, there was a sensation that something knowing and divine ceaselessly watched from beyond the dark sky.

"It's a journal. Some woman buried it. She lived here," Brant said. "Isn't that strange?"

Lloyd was leaning over now, continuing his massage, but moving his hands down onto Brant's chest rubbing gently.

"Why would anyone do that? What's she hiding?" Lloyd said. "Don't wake up any ghosts."

He let his hands move further, caressing Brant's stomach, then moving into his lap. Brant could not focus. The door to the living room opened.

"Good night," said Hem Raj. "I will see you for breakfast."

The door snapped shut. Brant was breathing heavily. Lloyd's hands remained, his face now close to Brant's, his lips kissing playfully. Brant took a deep breath and turned his face, seeking his husband's mouth. He let the journal slip to the ground, an offering to the sky and those divine falling back now in repose. Lloyd kissed him, then guided him up and into the house.

❧

Hem Raj had made the bed for them before retiring for the day. He had chosen a set of blood red sheets, the shade brutal against the starkness of their white house with its white walls. Brant undressed and lay on top of the sheet, his skin as pale as the house itself, like milk spilled on copper. There was an en-suite bathroom where Lloyd was noisily showering. He was singing but Brant did not recognize the song, nor could he make out the words. His husband was often very happy.

Hem Raj had installed black-out shades over the one large window which looked out onto the backyard. There was no light in the room, only that which came from the bathroom. The shower shut off and then that light, leaving the room much darker than Brant expected. It shot a momentary thrill through his body, as if he were facing danger in the black stillness, cast into some strange and foreboding new wilderness. Which of course Delhi was.

He heard Lloyd coming out of the bathroom. He was moving slowly and silently toward the bed. Brant barely made out his shape, saw more a hulking shadow creeping toward him. Their lovemaking was still very thrilling. It had not waned over the years. Brant sometimes thought of it as ferocious, the way the two of them got at one another.

Lloyd inched toward the end of the bed and Brant could make him out more clearly, his naked skin wet from the shower, his longish dark hair swept back. He brought a knee then another up onto the end of the bed and knelt there, thrusting his chest forward his breath the only sound. Brant's excitement was rising in a nearly uncomfortable and impatient way, knowing his body would soon be covered by Lloyd's.

Lloyd was aroused and Brant was tempted to sit up and crawl toward his husband but he waited, knowing it would be better to linger in this wordless state of anticipation, letting Lloyd come to him, to get fully on top of him and smother him with his bulk. The first feeling of that weight pressing on his body - nearly immobilizing him - was the point when he would lose control surrendering to his own deep place of instinct and desire.

As Lloyd crept closer Brant reached out his arms. He gasped as Lloyd crawled on top of him bringing that smothering comfort of legs-on-legs chest-on-chest. Brant cried out with pleasure holding onto his husband's back tightly bringing him closer, but pulling forward a rushing memory, a fast glimpse of that other man, the only other man he had tasted since he and Lloyd had started dating six years ago, the lusty shopkeeper in Cold Spring.

Lloyd now went for his open mouth, kissing. Drops of sweat fell from Lloyd's face and wide shoulders in the heat. Brant pressed his mouth on his husband's sweaty shoulder tasting, his hands gripping Lloyd's full muscular ass, unable to banish the memory of that other man the way he'd sloppily kissed him, and Brant could not contain his escalating excitement, as Lloyd ran his hand down the side of his body.

Brant was lost, dazed with lust. He welcomed a wickedness, a secret that felt delicious and taboo as Lloyd reached down and began to fondle him, teasing and manipulating him. In the rising fever pitch Brant felt his husband everywhere on him and he heard his moans and he felt the lusty specter of Cold Spring too and he could not delineate between the two men now in his mind, both pushing him quickly and greedily toward a rising ferocity and too he glimpsed, as if hovering above, the powerful visage of the monkey god.

Chapter 7

Hem Raj pulled his sleek black SUV into a small parking lot. The ground was a dull, stained concrete, multiple cracks forming lines like earthquake faults at several points across the lot, two merging and pointing to the front of a squat structure. The monkey temple.

There were small piles of rocks and rubble scattered around the area. It was as if something ancient had long ago fallen, bits of that history lingering indestructible.

There was an empty rickshaw lying on its side, and three heavy-set men in robes sitting in a circle on the ground.

Hem Raj had mentioned the temple that morning in his list of places to visit and Brant knew it was a sign. He'd had several odd lusty dreams about Hanuman and was sure it was a lingering curse summoned in Cold Spring. He wanted the memory of that transgression to die.

There was nothing to indicate this was a temple, other than three strands of lights stretching taut from the front of the place to a light pole across the way. Everything was a ghastly gray. He stepped out of the vehicle. Hem Raj waved him toward the trio of men who smiled broadly but remained seated.

"Give them your shoes," Hem Raj said.

Brant did as he was told, and Hem Raj gave the men rupees.

"This way," Hem Raj said.

Inside was a wide dank room, a concrete floor, a few stray raggedy looking men seated on red pillows. Around the edges and dead center toward the back were a series of golden statues of various sizes, varied depictions of the monkey god.

Brant was drawn to the largest rendition of Hanuman at the far side of the room. He moved toward it. Hem Raj lingered near the door.

It was a life-sized version of the statue he had seen in Cold Spring. But to Brant it was more grotesque. The figure was deeply golden bending down and resting on one knee with the other knee thrust forward as if taking a step. His legs were massive, large muscles straining, finely detailed with veins. It was as if a powerfully built man would at any moment burst through the golden patina. Hanuman wore tight red shorts and a thick blue woven belt which had a wide sash hanging straight down between his legs. It brushed his mighty thighs and touched the floor. He wore a very large V-shaped crown. His eyes were black and penetrating.

But the most startling thing, something Brant had not seen in Cold Spring, was the creature's chest. It was ripped open in the center. Hanuman was holding the sides of his blood-tinged flesh apart, revealing inside him, peering out, two women, one blue and one golden. The women's eyes were wide, mouths open and Brant imagined a soft growling, a sound that merged pain and ecstasy. He shuddered and abruptly stepped away, running into a person behind him. He turned and the man continued forward disregarding him, kneeling at Hanuman. The man began to chant. It was the only sound.

Brant moved quickly toward Hem Raj. There was no relief here.

Chapter 8

Miriam is an absolute fake. I've never been so fooled by anyone in my life. What a riot. I'd been after her about getting out for weeks. I told her I was sick to death of sitting at home. And then finally one night she told me she was taking me to try something new. Another side of Delhi.

"Are you sure?" she said to me. She had a sly look that was not like her. I should have known something was up. But I was certain she was a big bore.

"Yes I'm sure Miriam," I said, watching her try on a new pale orange lipstick, cross her legs on my couch, and smile. "Don't say I didn't warn you," she said. Which made me fume. As if I were the dull one. The innocent.

She took me to a part of town I'd never seen. We went into a basement. It was crowded and smoky and lined with people. Lots of men, some in uniform, but American women too and many Indian men. I knew right off it was a loose place but before I could say anything Miriam had scooted off to the end of the bar and was hanging onto a man I couldn't quite make out. He appeared to be very tall. I made my way over. The music was loud and the scene was not like anything I'd seen in Delhi. By the time I got to her, Miriam was busy kissing the fellow. She turned and said something like "get a drink" – it was very loud, I remember that. I think she shouted again. "You had to find out some time. Don't tell me you're surprised."

She turned back. He was Indian. They kissed for a while

then she turned to face me.

"You wanted a thrill," she said. "You want gin?"

I nodded. She leaned across the bar and her friend smiled at me. He had a large mouth and big white even teeth. I waited for my drink and was glad it was coming. I had felt so superior to Miriam, but here she'd been playing me.

It was a thrill to be out but it was odd what happened that night. I can't quite sort it out. I thought I knew what was what, and thought I was going to stay busy pulling something out of Miriam and stay who I was. Well that's done for. I've changed. Because while she was off in the ladies' room I kissed her friend. He didn't kiss me. I moved straight up to him, there at the end of that crowded smoky bar, and I kissed him smack on the lips. Fast before she got back. And I will see him again. I'm sure of it. So my dearest diary or whatever the hell you are – my threat of doing something rash came true! Prophetic!

I don't have anyone but Miriam to talk to so it's all going down on these pages. I'll spill everything.

Chapter 9

Jasmine was wearing a very short, white silk negligee. He had a pink ribbon tied around his neck and a jet black short-cropped wig with a fringe of bang. The lighting was spectacular, a soft pink glow framing him on the bed. They did not have long to talk.

"I have a private in 15," Jasmine said. "A new guy."

Brant had asked Jasmine for an emergency Skype check-in after his visit to the monkey temple and the new bits he'd read about Carol kissing a stranger. It had wrangled his nerves. He felt cursed.

Jasmine kept odd hours. Most of his on-screen fantasy clients were late night, which worked well with the ten-hour time difference between Delhi and the States.

"Who is the new one?" Brant said.

Jasmine was propping a set of pillows behind him on the bed, centering his screen image. Brant was in his yard with a computer on his lap. Hem Raj had left for the day and Lloyd was working late again.

"We don't have time sweetie," Jasmine said.

His voice was artificially sultry. He was a bit of a Method tart, so he needed to be fully in character. More than half of his income was from his OnlyFans page (the other cash from stray astrology readings, drag shows and some background film work).

"It's an omen," Brant said. "Carol says she's going to

have an affair then she kisses this man. Which is what I did. Then that horrible monkey god. It's all telling me something, right?"

Jasmine dabbed perfume on his neck.

"Can they smell you?" Brant said.

"You'd be surprised."

"It can't be a coincidence," Brant said. "It can't be good."

"Mercury is in retrograde. Are you reading the daily astrology report I send?"

Brant sighed.

"No."

"Well listen to me. Hard aspects between Venus and Pluto can bring on obsessive emotion. And I wrote about old flames coming back into our lives. I'll resend it."

"I just have this feeling these things came on after what I did," Brant said softly, quickly as if he were being spied on.

"This all may have *nothing* to do with Cold Spring. Don't do anything rash."

Brant gasped. Something rustled through a tree in the darkening yard.

"That's in the journal, those exact words. *Don't do anything rash*," Brant said.

"It's a common phrase," Jasmine said.

Jasmine took a deep breath in, holding it until Brant joined him. They both breathed out. She had been trying to convince him to meditate for months in addition to ceaselessly sharing columns about star movements, things going into retrograde, which Brant found baffling. He had always been wildly superstitious but found no solace in Jasmine's cosmic predictions.

29

"You sit tight. You are in another world and you are tense. Just sit still. And read what I send you. I'll dig around. Pam Gregory just put out something new."

There was a soft beeping noise.

"I can't be late. Our first call. Give me a little time and we'll talk again. Love you," Jasmine said.

Without warning the session ended. Brant closed the laptop. He was very unsettled, but he trusted his friend. Jasmine had held his hand through several rough spots. He was his best man at the wedding. Brant tended to act too quickly and did things he regretted. He needed to be patient, to wait for their next call. To calm the fuck down.

Brant looked out at the yard. Even in the dark, the flowers were bright. They had multiplied since he and Hem Raj had been gardening. The tilting tree stood tall its leaves no longer tipped black. He certainly had done something right since he'd gotten to Delhi. And maybe there was a good reason he had found the journal. Maybe the answer was there, with Carol.

Chapter 10

They sat very low to the ground, on stout, fabric-covered stools facing each other across a wooden table. They were at the famed Bukhara restaurant. The walls were a deep red stone. Chefs in cylindrical white hats stoked flames in the open-concept kitchen. It was crowded and scented so heavily with cumin, clove and cardamom that Brant tasted the spices on his tongue. The food so far was dal with beans in earth fired bowls and drinks in rustic copper cups. It was Punjabi cuisine.

Lloyd was beaming. He had pulled strings to get them a much-coveted center table. It reminded Brant of the night Lloyd proposed. He'd gone to great lengths then too.

"This is such a perfect time for us," Lloyd said loudly. "In Delhi."

Now, as then, Brant felt incapable of rising to his husband's giddy heights. He only wished he could fall into the glistening light of it all, but he could not. He felt restless.

"Tell me what you've been doing while I work," Lloyd said.

Lloyd hunched slightly forward, balancing his broad body on the small stool, his muscular legs sprawled wide open. He smiled, dipped naan into a bowl of dal, ate it, then licked his fingers one by one. There was a sensual Viking-like roughness to it that aroused Brant. Lloyd looked up awaiting an answer.

"We went to the monkey temple today," Brant said.

Lloyd plucked another piece of naan from a golden copper plate and shoved it into his mouth.

"Yes?" he said.

Brant had an urge to lean forward and kiss him but he was afraid. This was India, not New York City. All the guidebooks stressed the danger of public affection.

A rotund server in a striped costume and turban laid a plate of buttery spiced chicken on the table for them to share. He smiled at Brant and waited as if Brant were meant to taste the dish like a drinker tastes that first mouthful of a fine wine. Brant reached over and lifted a piece of the bird which had been coated in a slick batter. He put it into his mouth. The flavor was incredibly rich, a swarm of spices and something deeper, earthier.

"Yes," Brant said to the waiter. "Very good."

The server nodded and left. Lloyd tasted.

"How's that book you're reading?" Lloyd said.

Brant sat up startled, as if Carol had stepped out from shadow to touch his husband's shoulder. In the same moment, he noticed a woman near the restaurant's door in a burgundy dress. She disappeared down a narrow hallway that led to the bathroom.

"It's a journal. It's so strange that I found it in our garden."

Lloyd lifted another piece of chicken, leaned over offering it. Brant opened his mouth and took it in. It felt a bit daring, but it was something Lloyd liked to do. He imagined Carol watching.

"What's it about?"

Brant paused, considering the journal's early revelations. He wished the woman in the burgundy dress would re-emerge and nod with approval.

"She lived in our house with her husband. But she has a funny friend."

"Well, what happens?" Lloyd said. "Is it dull?"

Brant felt stung by the suggestion.

"Oh no she just went to a dark bar and kissed a man," Brant said with excitement.

"Didn't you say she was married," Lloyd said. "So, she's cheating on her husband?"

As if summoned to deliver a verdict, the woman in the burgundy dress darted from around the corner then crossed the restaurant near their table. Brant felt flushed. Lloyd had said it so matter of factly. She's cheating. She strayed. She broke a sacred trust.

Brant sat silently. Lloyd looked at him, waiting.

"What's wrong, did you cheat on me?" he said with a smile.

In a flashing moment of panic, Brant was struck with a dizzying vision of an elaborate board game, some unholy merging of Ouija and childhood. It was hovering above him in the restaurant. Golden figurines tripping across a steaming black board, stepping too quickly, all fated and unavoidable, all predestined and done, really. Done since Cold Spring, he thought.

Lloyd was staring at him. The silence had been too long, too telling. Brant's eyes were glazed, his head swimming. He began to tremble.

"Brant?"

Brant was frozen in fear. He was falling into a deep confusion. Lloyd frowned, waited, then glared at him.

"Brant what the hell," Lloyd began. "What the hell."

Lloyd's face was turning crimson. He was not a person to get mad, certainly not in public. He stood up abruptly and his napkin fell to the floor. The rotund server scurried over, and Lloyd said loudly, "Leave it."

Brant did not stand. He thought if he stayed very still, Lloyd would sit back down.

"It's a journal, a story," Brant said, hearing the weakness in his voice.

"What did you do Brant?" Lloyd said.

Lloyd did not sit down. Brant noticed his husband's fists were clenched. He knew what he had to do. Speak loudly, quickly, deny it, make a joke. How ridiculous this all is, are you insane?

But he could not open his mouth, it was sewn tightly shut. He had kept things hidden, but he had never blatantly lied to his husband. He realized he did not know how. Theirs was a love so innately trusting, so unforced, a bold lie felt sinful.

The moments ticked past. Time slowed in a terrible way. The longer he stayed silent, the stronger the inability to escape. There was no way out. He could only say it as it was.

"In Cold Spring. That day. I was with someone. Just once."

Lloyd did not move from the spot he had planted himself in. The napkin laid crumpled near his feet like something dead. He did not speak. He took in a deep breath, then let out a sound so foreign, so guttural, loud and frightening that

Brant leapt up trying to grab his hand. But before he could Lloyd fell back, away from him, as if his touch were acid and as Brant began to speak, to plead in useless language, Lloyd turned toward the startled waiter and moved solidly, soldier-like and quickly out of the restaurant.

Brant stood for several moments, too frightened to pursue him, still reeling from the aching noise his husband had made, that horrible sound that *he* had brought forth.

The rotund waiter was staring at him strangely and Brant slowly sat down. The waiter approached the table. He stood there, waiting, studying Brant, not smiling, as if Brant were meant to say something to offer an explanation.

Stricken and numbed, Brant could think of nothing to do, but pick up pieces of the chicken and eat it, slowly, until the awful man finally went away, and he was left absolutely and utterly alone.

Part 2

Chapter 11

Brant knew their house was not far. He had some money, a fistful of rupees, but he did not know their worth so he didn't want to fuss with a cab. He would walk home. This would quiet his mind. He would figure out what to say so Lloyd understood that the tryst meant nothing. That it would never happen again. If that didn't work he would beg for his forgiveness.

The restaurant was located in a luxury hotel. Brant swept past the bellhops standing at alert at the grand front entrance, men in starched white uniforms with starched white pill box hats and bright white gloves.

He didn't dare look at anyone. He was burning with an unshakeable shame. He felt they were judging him with every step, noticing this strange dirty American fleeing alone. He turned once, imagining the woman in the burgundy dress was following him, or the server in the turban. He had to get away quickly.

There was a wide lawn in front of the property and past that in the distance, a short curling road leading out to the main thoroughfare. He moved across the lawn expecting someone to shout at him to stop but they did not. There were strange animal sounds. Cawing, crying, shrill sounds. It was very hot.

The distance to the road was further than he imagined. He moved more quickly but it was as if the lawn ahead of him was expanding with each step, while at the same time the glimmering lights from the hotel were fast disappearing behind him swallowed by a permanent darkness. He stopped to catch his breath. He looked up at the night sky. It was not a comforting sky. It was vacant and black like a non-existing thing, not at all ancient and spiritual as he wanted it to be, as he wanted everything in Delhi to be. He was stricken with a knowing that *he* was the foreign thing. And he realized too, looking first angrily and then with awe at the night sky, that he expected all life to serve his needs. Even the heavens above owed him comfort.

He began moving again, listening for the sound of traffic on the thoroughfare, desperate to get away from the brushing sounds of the trees lining the lawn and the cawing night animals. He began to run.

At the road, there was a strip of grass facing a busy, honking four-lane. He wondered if he in his crisp white linen clothing stood out as much as the bellhops did in the lobby. A small, motorized rickshaw with a flimsy fabric roof pulled off the road stopping next to him. Hem Raj had told him this was a tuk tuk, something he should never get into because they were tipsy and precarious. A shirtless, thin young man with a spot of black hair at the very top of his head waved him into the vehicle calling "Come, come!"

Brant was relieved to hear English, not Hindi. He surely had enough rupees to get the few blocks home and the contraption looked sturdy enough for the trip. He stepped up into the tuk tuk sitting on the hard wooden seat. He began to speak, but the driver shot the tiny rickshaw directly across the road through rushing and weaving traffic, taking a hard turn away from the direction Brant was sure they needed to go.

"No," Brant said. "Wait."

They were moving at a rapid clip. Cars, motorcycles and trucks crammed with people were speeding past them in both directions honking and overwhelming his thin voice.

"Wait!" he yelled again into a hot wind.

The driver began to laugh wildly, then turned directly around, ignoring the road ahead and smiling.

"I know! I know. India Gate."

As he turned back, he swerved around a slower car and the tuk tuk lilted as if it would indeed tip over.

"Good time," the driver screamed with glee.

Brant clutched the metal bars on either side of the seat. He did not panic. He was not being kidnapped, rather forced into some tourist night tour. He would get out of the thing as soon as they stopped. It was simply a misadventure, the kind he and Lloyd would laugh about at a dinner party in New York.

As they approached a circular roundabout, trailing the edge of a small park that divided the diverging pathways, they came to an abrupt halt. There was something blocking the way. He heard a lowing sound. A cow.

He considered getting out, but there were vehicles all around them. They were honking ceaselessly. People were yelling, some laughing and many were staring directly at him and pointing.

Coming toward their tuk tuk, walking through the traffic, was a large curvaceous woman in a deep red sari. She lifted her arms in the air as she moved revealing a dozen golden bracelets from wrist to elbow. She was barefoot. As she approached, gazing intently at Brant, she held out a hand palm open and began shouting in Hindi. The driver barked at the stranger, and she hissed at him, still approaching. Brant stiffened, bristling with fear and a steely haughtiness that broke apart his humanity thinking *keep your distance you dirty beggar I am a white man and you best not touch me.* Yet shadowed beneath that was a deeper fear, a truer fear that said without Lloyd, without his husband's money and protection, he was meritless and could be devoured, spat out, and quickly forgotten. He could end up like her.

Finally, the traffic began to move but before they veered off, the woman smiled at Brant lifting her arms in the air again, thrusting her hips side to side and tilting back her head. It was as if she were an incarnation of his sexual sins, a Hindu demon taunting him.

"I need to get home," Brant shouted as they sped onward.

The driver made another sharp turn, darting around a truck and racing straight to their destination. The India Gate. He halted in front of the monument and hopped out. He was barefoot. He pointed.

"India Gate," he said, then folded his arms smiling with pride.

It was impressive in the distance, lit at its square top with green, white and orange, the whole thing anchored onto heavy columns with granite, grace and grandeur. It was brilliant to look at, and strong.

Brant stepped out of the tuk tuk taking in the monument's steadying force. It calmed him, but in that calm he acknowledged that he had likely wrecked at least a piece of what was truly good and solid in his life, the thing he thought was impenetrable and forever beautiful. He began to weep softly.

The driver, frowning now, slowly approached Brant one hand outstretched. Brant did not move, he only stared ahead at the startling granite apparition, reaching into his pocket for his few rupees.

Chapter 12

Brant woke sweating. A ceiling fan spun sluggishly above the bed, cutting at dead air. Lloyd had been sleeping deeply when he'd arrived home. Brant sat up touching the sunken imprint on the pillow where Lloyd had laid his head. He hadn't heard him get up. He wiped his brow. His silk pajamas were damp with perspiration. The heat felt stale and relentless.

He padded across the floor out into the long wide main room, then into the kitchen. Hem Raj sat at an oblong kitchen table smiling, his hands folded. There was a blue envelope on the table. There was a china cup in a saucer with coffee. Brant sat. The blue envelope had his name on it. The handwriting was Lloyd's.

"Where is he?" Brant said.

"Gone early Sir," Hem Raj said, rising and moving toward the refrigerator.

"I will make whatever you desire," he said. "I am prepared."

Brant tore at the envelope. The message was simple.

"Gone to Agra. Business. Will be in touch."

There was a central office in Agra, and several of Lloyd's Indian co-workers lived there. It was a hub. It was five hours by car and on the way to the Taj Mahal. He folded the note and put it back in its blue envelope. He touched the letters on the front spelling his name.

"A western omelet?" Hem Raj said, waiting.

"All right," Brant said.

They had planned to go to Agra together and see the Taj Mahal. It was agreed upon.

He did not move his hand from the envelope. He did not want to let go of it. There had to be more hidden under the letters, coded into the texture of the blue paper. Things could not collapse this swiftly. They were a married couple and couples worked things out.

He was afraid to call Lloyd or make any movement. Lloyd may not answer the call. Each step forward could bring him closer to a terrible end.

"What have I done?" Brant said softly, covering his face with one hot hand.

Hem Raj had his back to him and was busy cooking as if the day were moving along at a fine pace. Brant stood abruptly.

"I have to do something," he said.

Hem Raj finished the dish, plated and served it.

"Please eat," Hem Raj said, smiling.

Brant looked at the plate. He sat and began to eat since he was very hungry, and his body was weak, depleted from sweating all night.

"My wife is at our home in the mountains. It is far. She waits knowing I will come back," Hem Raj said.

Brant looked up at Hem Raj. The man they had hired to keep their house, to drive him around. His role of service was so anchored in his body that it had until this moment kept his presence in slight perpetual shadow. Lloyd's departure had brought him fully into the light. He was

45

looking at Brant, and there was deep compassion there and something else he did not understand.

"What will happen?" Brant said.

Looking down, Hem Raj said softly, "Inshallah."

"What?" Brant said.

"As God wills," Hem Raj said, smiling.

"I don't know what to do," Brant said.

And that was true. He felt as if he were drowning, sinking deeper into an abyss of contradictory feelings that he did not understand. All he could imagine was packing his bag and going back to the States. But that was not right.

He was an adulterer, abandoned in a foreign land. It had been his fault, but the punishment did not fit the crime. It seemed implausible as if a cherished plate he had been holding firmly suddenly smashed to pieces and he did not know how he let it slip. It was in his hand and then it was on the floor destroyed. There was nothing in between.

"The garden is in need of your care," Hem Raj said. "And today we can visit my favorite temple. That is what you will do. Just for now."

At that, Hem Raj stood and moved out of the kitchen.

"I will lay out your clothes," he shouted from the other room. "We will get started before the heat gets too strong."

Brant felt very much like a child being instructed by a parent. He thought again of calling Lloyd but he was afraid. The closeness they had was now stretched taut and everything from the sunshine days felt flimsy and far off. He had lost his mother, and now he may lose Lloyd. The hurt was too deep to comprehend.

He got up and went to Hem Raj. He would follow the

gentle voice, the soft suggestions and that would give him balance, and he would regain himself and together they would know what to do.

Chapter 13

As they climbed the steep red sandstone staircase toward the Lal Mandir temple's arched entrance, Brant was struck with a feeling of divinity. Not his own, nothing of the sort, he was feeling quite the opposite, quite evil for having created a seemingly unmendable fracture between him and Lloyd. Following Hem Raj, ascending in the heat toward a rhythmic chanting, he had a distinct and unnerving sensation that he was stepping *into* something momentary and full and *away* from something enduring and empty.

"The oldest Jain temple in Delhi," Hem Raj said softly. Then, "Leave your shoes."

Brant released his leather Prada loafers to a squat, dusty-looking old man as Hem Raj laid down rupees. They entered the temple, but stopped just past the entrance, observing. It was the size of a small courtyard and crowded with worshippers. The walls and ceiling were adorned with strips of gold and covered with intricately painted depictions of what appeared to be golden cities. Throughout were statues of deities. They all were seated, legs crossed, stone idols cast in shades of white, gray, blue and green. They were smooth, appearing sexless to Brant, though the eyes were brightly painted and feminine.

Brant believed in fate and miracles, and he felt within these walls a tangible feeling of shared devotion. He was both excited and a bit afraid.

There was no one like him in the temple, no tourists that he could see. It was all local people. Some of the men wore smocks, while quite a few of the women were draped in bright silk fabrics of red, orange and yellow. He did not feel part of the scene, but he did not feel rejected by it. He felt folded into it and tolerated.

Brant did not move any deeper into the temple. Hem Raj waited at his side, then smiled and sat, indicating he should do the same. Brant sat on the cool floor, trying awkwardly at first to cross his legs but giving into his favorite side saddle (as if he were poised at a picnic listening to a story). From that vantage point, he was slightly lower, which felt right, and he could watch the worshippers' movements, their ease. In the distance, came the cry of a bird. He looked to Hem Raj, who spoke softly.

"There is next to the temple, a hospital for birds. Very old."

He smiled, then lowered his head and shut his eyes.

For a moment Brant shut his eyes too and listened intently to the voices, wanting to recognize a phrase or prayer or intention. It began to sound like music. For a moment, he imagined Lloyd stepping through one of the decorative archways lining the walls, taking his hand as they began to dance.

There was another cry of a bird, then the sound of shouting from the street, and opening his eyes Brant thought of his shoes. He couldn't be sure how long they'd been sitting there, likely only a few minutes, but he became afraid that his expensive shoes would be gone. He also became acutely aware that he was barefoot.

Hem Raj was standing now, nodding to him as if his panic had taken shape and shaken the man out of his momentary ecstasy in the temple. Hem Raj moved toward the door and Brant followed him quickly filled with a terrific and sudden regret that he was yanking himself away too soon, rushing back to a world he knew so well, a world lacking the capacity to illicit any real awe.

As they stepped into a blinding sun, he felt his phone vibrate. A text from Lloyd: "Sorting things out. Back in a week or so."

Near the stone stairway leading away, Hem Raj was holding his shoes high in the air, waiting for him to claim them.

Chapter 14

She passed him to me. That's how Miriam put it. "I'll pass him to you." Like an hors d'oeuvre or a martini. She's done with Ajan. Time for a new lover. Another handsome Indian man, I guess. She's a devil, that one. I see now I was her cover. Stick with good old Carol. She's respectable. I laughed and acted like I didn't care, but I sure do. I'm glad Miriam is done with Ajan. Our kiss at the club woke something in me. Passion, I suppose. I'm too young to stop having sex and Gerald is drifting further away. It's becoming more like a business arrangement, our marriage, which mother always insisted was the best case. I don't think he's seeing anyone else. I sometimes wonder if he has a hidden desire. Men maybe, or something else he hides away from me.

I'm seeing Ajan this week…

Brant saw scribbled in the margin: *Clean green silk dress. More gin. Write mother.*

His laptop, which sat on the bed next to him, lit up with a reminder. It was time for his Skype call with Jasmine. He had texted him about the situation with Lloyd's disappearing to Agra and Jasmine suggested they talk. He set aside Carol and brought the computer into his lap logging in and bringing his friend to life.

After a moment, from dull screen to camera, Jasmine appeared. His head was shaved. His eyebrows were gone. A small child with red hair ran behind him on screen.

"What was that?" Brant said.

Jasmine ignored the question. A loudspeaker announced a flight delay. The child darted by again.

"How far is Agra?" Jasmine said.

Brant leaned closer to the screen.

"Where are you going?" he asked.

"Geneva. I'm at JFK. I have a client."

Jasmine wore a sharply tailored blue suit with a blue shirt with tiny ruffles down the front.

"Will you Skype me when you get there?" Brant said. "I'm worried."

Jasmine arched what would be an eyebrow, tilting his head forward slightly. It was a movement Brant knew well. His friend was going to "school" him.

"I have a job sweetie. Don't deflect."

Jasmine leaned in a bit further, so his face was closer to the screen.

"This thing with Lloyd is not good," Jasmine said. "You should have waited to talk to me. Listen to me closely."

Again, the red-haired child ran behind Jasmine. It disturbed Brant. He wondered if it really was a child, or some creature, phantom or vision. Another sign. He was overly tired. He lay his head back on the pillow and shut his eyes to focus as he listened.

"Go ahead," Brant said.

"I want you to do what I say. Three things. Threes are important. First, go to Agra. Go find Lloyd."

Brant opened his eyes and sat up. The laptop fell off into the bed covers, Jasmine sinking away. He recovered it. Jasmine continued unfazed.

"Second. I am texting you the number of a friend of mine. Mendah. She lives in Delhi. She is insanely rich and very smart. You need a connection. Call her. Meet her. And thirdly, keep reading that journal."

Carol sat open, as if listening between scrawled pages. She was by his side where he'd left off reading. He imagined the pages rustled with delight.

"She is your guide sweetie. I know you think it's all about Cold Spring but it's not. The longer you hold that chain around your heart, the further you're going to drift from what is coming to you. The true revelation is in that book you literally dug up. Pay attention."

Jasmine sat back again. He smiled and shook his head.

"My little sister. You're going to be all right."

Brant stared at the screen, at his dearest friend, comforted though still afraid.

"I have to go," Jasmine said, putting two fingers to his lips, then sending off a kiss.

"But what are you doing in Geneva?" Brant said.

"Don't worry. I'll be fine. Love you."

And with that, he disappeared.

Chapter 15

The four-hour trip to Agra was all freeway. A straight shot. It appeared to Brant as a blazing gray wasteland. The only break from the fast-blurring concrete was an occasional set of tents on the side of the road, some with small fires going. After passing the first, Brant leaned forward from the back seat, toward Hem Raj who was driving.

"Are those Shanti towns?" he said.

There was a long pause, then Hem Raj began.

"In Hindi, Shanti means peace," he said, his eyes on the road ahead. "Shanti is chanted three times to represent threefold peace in body, mind and spirit."

Brant sat back, startled. Another sign. Jasmine had given him three tasks. He had said threes were an important part of the journey. He opened Carol's journal, which was on the seat beside him. He had folded the page over where he'd left off. She'd made a margin note about cleaning a green silk dress.

I'll have to wear the yellow chiffon tonight to the club. Dinner with Gerald. Whopee. Gerald is so clueless. Last night he gave me one of those smiles, the "you poor thing" smile and said "I know it's hard being stuck in the house. We'll go to the club." As if that antiseptic place - oh I don't know what to call it. That draberie. As if it could ever be a thrill. But I best play my role with Gerald. Just in case. I certainly don't want to be sued for divorce. Branded as the wicked adulteress. Would he even care enough?

I may not show up to see Ajan. I told Miriam he asked me to meet him and she smiled, something she doesn't do much at all. "Really?" she said. I knew it was a dare. She thinks I'll back out. Good old simple Carol. Well, we'll see. Oh hell I think I will show up. The place he told me to meet him is called Kwality. I guess that means quality. I doubt it. Ha. I have the address.

Again, in the margin, this time written sideways: *Get postcards. Letter, mother, quit stalling!*

Chapter 16

As they entered Agra Brant drew in a quick breath. The wide street, bordered by ramshackle huts, heaps of rubble, squatting young men and emaciated cows, was immediately grotesque and captivating. Brant began to roll down the car window to see more clearly but Hem Raj spoke up.

"No sir, no, the monkeys will come."

Brant did as he was told, pressing his face to the dusty car window as they crept along moving deeper into the city. It was nothing like Delhi and to Brant it seemed more like a town which had been ravaged by war or pestilence. Many of the low cement structures were crumbling. The people crowding the edges of the street, all staring at the smart black vehicle passing through, were dressed in ragged clothing. Monkeys nibbled at things on wires dripping close to the ground. Bony dogs drowsed. Flies circled. Brant could not imagine the Taj Mahal was anywhere near this disturbing place.

Around the next turn, there was, however, an elaborate gate, and through that, set back a bit was a shimmering thing. It was the hotel. As they approached it, Brant turned his body quickly to look back at the sordid street behind but could see nothing past the high gate. It was as if the squalor, just a hundred feet away, had ceased to exist. He wondered if Carol had seen the Taj Mahal, had been to this place.

Hem Raj opened the SUV door and smiled. Brant

stepped out toward the hotel entrance, where sharply dressed bellhops guided him inside. The marble-floored lobby was immense. At its center was a massive chandelier. From the vaulted ceiling, frosted circular bulbs hung from narrow brass pendants at different levels, forming a large V shape. It illuminated a black marble table featuring a vase with striking, exotic blood-red bulbs. To either side of this centering piece were dark rattan welcome desks, where elegantly dressed women stood. Beyond the lobby (and a second identically decked out lobby area) were ceiling height windows looking out toward a garden rich in color and bloom.

He went to the check-in desk. The immense wall behind the desk was covered with glossy blue tiles. Efficient and gracious, the woman handed him his room key along with a note in a red envelope. Hem Raj was waiting under the chandelier.

A bit dazed, Brant sought out a couch in the second lobby area. He had texted Lloyd he was coming but only received back the hotel address. He had hoped Lloyd would meet him upon arrival, that they would begin to piece things back together. Instead, the note:

At an unexpected business meeting at our Gurgaon office. Out tonight. Will join you in the morning to see the Taj Mahal. Lloyd.

Brant folded the note and put it into his pocket. He had hoped for so much more, but he was brightened by the fact that they would be together in the morning. Hem Raj approached. He smiled at Brant kindly.

"Will you be staying in tonight?" Hem Raj said.

Brant sighed, grateful for the suggestion, and grateful that he did not have to explain anything to Hem Raj. He nodded.

"I will see you in the morning then," Hem Raj said.

"Are you staying here?" Brant said.

"No."

Hem Raj bowed, then left. Brant wondered where he went once he veered back onto that chaotic dirty street. But he had not yet learned the proper questions to ask, or the right tone to set when their conversation veered away from anything other than the rudimentary. Or rather, anything other than his own needs.

Chapter 17

I let him –

There was a jarring mark as if the ink had smeared to the edge of the page.

Then a few x marks. A drawn heart, that had a line through it. Then below that:

I have you hidden. Under my slips. That was too close. Gerald crept up like a damn cat. What are you writing? His small talk is so obvious. Still, I was absolutely quaking. So now you are hidden, and I'll have to burn you when we leave Delhi. Or bury you in the back yard. In that horrible little garden plot. Gerald suggested that I plant flowers or vegetables. He's clueless. I'm not a fucking farmer.

So, that was last week. I haven't written here since Gerald spooked me. I also haven't seen Ajan since he touched me like… Let him touch me yes but... Did Miriam tell him where I live? I can't imagine that. I'm on the brink of telling her all about it. The sordid details. I want to see him again. I do. Where do I find him? Each day I'm getting a little more…what's the word, desperate. And after what he did to me! I'm going mad. That's obvious. I keep running the moment through my mind. Hoping I will dream it, feel it that way. But I don't.

I met him at Kwality. It was small and he was there waiting. In the back. Hands folded. His hair combed back. It's very black. I looked around like I didn't see him because I was a bit shocked to see how good-looking he was in the light. I expected much less. Most people look better in a dark bar. Not him. I let my eyes land on him, and he smiled. He had on a short sleeve white shirt that hugged his muscular arms. Gerald's arms are like sticks.

I waved and stood there like seeing an old friend at a lunch spot back home. Looking stupid, I'm sure. But he was just so damned good looking. Striking. And that made me nervous. I walked slowly to his table, then sat across from him and right away he took my hand which I thought was bold. But I didn't pull away. I was trembling. It had been forever since anyone held my hand or looked at me that way, like I was…what? A piece of fruit. Oh that sounds dumb.

The place was empty. He started to stroke the inside of my palm. Like he would tell my fortune. He smiled all the time. We had beer. His English was halting but decipherable. Short and to the point which I rather enjoyed. I was pretty well gone right away. We only kissed that once in the bar but I was pretty well oh what did we used to say? Smitten. He wanted to take a walk.

The street in front of the place was by a market. We walked a block then he turned into an alley then there was a wide entryway with a staircase going way up. He said roof. I followed him, well wait, by then he had taken my hand again and there were so many swarming people all the time. During our walk. I still can't get used to so many things, so many people. He led me up then stopped. We were on a small landing between staircases. A shirtless man with a shaving razor darted past us.

Ajan smiled. He touched my hair. He pulled me to him. I can't say I didn't want that kiss. I think that's when I really lost myself. Me, in a dirty stairway. A public stairway. Kissing this beautiful yes, this beautiful Indian man. Then he ran his

60

hands…

An abrupt stop. The page was empty.

Brant sat up in bed. Had Gerald walked in on her? He reached to a pen on his bedside table. He hesitated then he wrote on Carol's page:

If Lloyd had walked in. In Cold Spring. If Lloyd had walked…in. If he would just walk in now…

He stopped, excited and afraid. Lloyd had, in a way, walked in, because Brant had told him what happened. He looked at the journal, not wanting to shut it, not wanting to go to bed alone in this sad hotel room. He'd inserted himself into her story. And that made the loneliness bearable.

Chapter 18

Together, Brant and Lloyd had seen many impressive temples, mosques and even a red fort in Delhi but now, coming around a sharp corner at dawn with Hem Raj, he witnessed vividly in the distance a thing to be reckoned with, this that could not be ignored as it overcame the sky and stopped his breath, this solid yet floating mausoleum that willed him to bow (he did not) and certainly to stop moving. For several moments there was nothing else, no one else, just the glowing white dome with finial which was not of this world, not in the least - rather anchored in the air, ethereal and eternal, solid in the way of a cloud not of the hard glowing marble that it was. The Taj Mahal.

"Magnificent, yes?" Hem Raj said quietly.

Brant did not answer because he could not. He felt as if he were falling yet he could not move. He was transfixed. It was as if he had taken a very deep breath in and his body would not release it, would not allow this moment to pass.

There were no thoughts, only a feeling of weightlessness and a disorienting awe and then a reckoning of his absolute insignificance and so clearly that he was alone without Lloyd. Then at last, an exhaling rush of sadness and wonder, the loss of his mother, and the sense that he was settling back into the moment, and the brilliant mirage was done with him, having given him a glimpse of its grandeur before discarding him with the rest of humanity.

He knew he would never forget that first glimpse, nor that fact that he was without his husband, without Lloyd who had begged off ("detained in Gurgaon" the text said) but who in Brant's mind was now fully part of their growing distance, a more active player as he had rejected a moment that should not have been missed. No matter what had happened prior.

"Shall we sit," Hem Raj said, indicating a stone bench.

They sat on the bench facing the mausoleum. Brant, breathing evenly again, watched the crowd of Indian men and women moving slowly toward the massive thing. There were smaller domes on either side of the largest one this all atop a structure with identical archways everything symmetrical and softly glowing. It was hard to keep looking at, like some brilliant risen white sun that he could not look away from but that burned. The moment was tinged with a growing weariness; an aching sadness and he was tired of it. There was a very long pool, bordered by two walkways leading to the Taj Mahal.

"The pool gives a reflection," Hem Raj said. "Hawd al-Kawthar is that abundance promised to Muhammad."

"I want to go," Brant said, standing and turning away.

"We can go closer, inside," Hem Raj began. "There is so much more."

But Brant had already begun to walk toward the exit, knowing he could not look back because this was all wrong, the moment was no good, a momentum of dismantling had begun that he had to stop before it reached a terrible conclusion, or revealed to him that the end had already happened without his even bearing witness.

Chapter 19

It's been a while. I quit writing here. I was afraid. I lead two lives. With Ajan, and without Ajan. I have to tell Miriam. I have to confess. It's gone too far. I quit writing what he and I do because the words would scream at me to stop. To walk away before it's too late. But now…

The last time he brought another man. Just thinking of it thrills me. I'm ashamed. Who am I becoming! It's like I'm writing of someone else. Not me. But I want to see him now, this very minute. God I'm a goner. I'm going to write this down. If I can't tell Miriam out loud then she can read it. I'll hand this to her and run away. But I can't hide it away like it's not happening.

A month has gone by. The first time, in the stairway, I knew. I knew he was not a good man. A devil. But I didn't care. I felt powerful, knowing he wanted me. It's been so long since I've done anything with Gerald. I needed that. But I didn't expect the rest.

Each time we met, he pressed a little deeper and I felt myself sinking. The dark bar, then the ratty hotel room. An alley. Each time it felt like a tiny push further away from who I thought I was. I believed back then that I could still walk away. I could tell Miriam, call it a lark. Laugh. I even went one full week without seeing him. I thought about what I had with Gerald. He is a decent man. We have a good life. If I stop now, I thought. If I stop. It can all be just fine. Like it was before we ever came to

Delhi. I can go back to the old me.

It's funny about secrets. Desire. It's so tasty. That's a stupid word. I'm a stupid woman. To even be caught up in this with Ajan. But after a week, lying awake at night. I knew I'd see him again. I had changed. And I couldn't go back.

The night he brought the other man. Gerald was away. I knew I had time. I was at the hotel room; the desk clerk knew me since we'd been there twice before. I waited. On the bed. It was dark. I liked it like that. The street outside the window one floor down was busy, even very late. Loud voices.

They came in together, side by side. They stood in the doorway. The other man could have been his brother, same height, dark hair, well built. I knew what was going to happen. I knew but I sat still. The whole affair is like a drug. Just a little more this time.

They came in that way, side by side, then sat on the end of the bed where I was, on either side of me. They were like doubles of the same man, and I thought this isn't really much different from what we've done before. Not really. They are just two of the same. But I knew it was different. Still, I laid back on the bed. And that was that.

Brant woke at dawn. The journal lay open by his side. He'd fallen asleep reading it. Lloyd too was there on the other side of the journal, snoring. Brant wondered how it was he did not hear his husband come in, did not feel his body move onto the bed after his long absence. He closed the journal, like shutting out a light, imagining Carol had seen Lloyd before he had. That she had witnessed his return while he had slept through it.

Chapter 20

They were alone in the *Moonlight Garden*. It was not yet dawn and 105 degrees. Hem Raj had suggested that they make the stop before departing Agra. The garden, or *Mehtab Bagh*, stretched across the flood plains that lay at the bank of the Yamuna River. Across the narrow waterway shimmered the Taj Mahal.

There was no one around. It was too hot. The landscape, famed for its alternate perspective of the Taj Mahal, seemed flat, torn up and withered to Brant. Stretches of gray sandy soil then grass patches that pressed through with desperation. There was a brown wire fence dividing areas and a low brick wall facing the Yamuna with its mesmerizing view.

Brant and Lloyd sat on the wall. The white marble of the magnificent structure glowed in the pre-dawn, then as light came, the sun slowly rising, it began to gradually change. Brant stifled an urge to take Lloyd's hand. They had said very little to each other since Lloyd reappeared.

The central dome was now half in light, half in shadow and there was a glow behind the structure giving the illumination a soft redness. Brant took a deep breath, his mind blank. He waited.

"I didn't believe you," Lloyd finally said.

Lloyd was facing the river. His palms were flat on the wall. He spoke soft and low and Brant thought it might be the changing light, that vision, causing them both to fall into a dreamy lull.

"I thought it was a joke. I was waiting for you to finish the story. Then you didn't. That made it worse," Lloyd said.

"You left me alone," Brant said.

He turned to Lloyd and quickly brought his hands together, twining his fingers as if in prayer because he felt a need to hold onto something and there was nothing there.

"There was nothing. Just nothing," Brant said.

Lloyd finally turned to face him, and Brant saw immediately a deep weariness, a wide depth of sadness and desperation in his face and eyes as the sun now hitched higher and began to shed its harsh unforgiving light directly upon them like a judging deity.

"I was done with you," Lloyd said. "It was like it all went to shit."

Brant began to shake, as if chilled, despite the heat which brought on a steady sweat staining the collar of his shirt and under his arms. His mouth was moving but he was not forming words. Then finally:

"You can't," Brant said sharply.

He stood and threw himself at Lloyd, falling into him and grasping his thick neck, pressing his hot and sweaty face close. He began to cry, a loud ragged weeping, speaking in hard fragments, the sort of wail Lloyd had cut loose with at the restaurant, but harsher.

Lloyd stood abruptly pushing him away and Brant fell backwards. He sat on the ground looking up at his husband who was in full sunlight now, tall and broad his dark hair a bit wild. Brant suddenly noticed he was unshaven.

Lloyd stared at him, then slowly bent down to help him up and Brant grabbed him again, yanking him on top of him so they both lay in the dirt, finding his mouth, forcing a kiss, tasting his husband's tongue and not letting go, not pulling away, moving his lips to his salty sweaty cheek. Lloyd pressed both hands to the sides of Brant's face.

"Stop it!" he screamed.

Lloyd held Brant's hot face as a distant call to prayer began - a melody of some reckoning, something otherly and mysterious emanating from that grand white structure across the river. Finally, he kissed Brant's forehead, then leaning his back against the low stone wall, pulled him close.

"I came back," Lloyd said. "I'm here now."

Part 3

Chapter 21

A four-foot stone statue of the Hindu goddess Parvati rose as a striking centerpiece to bursting pale pink hibiscus, light orange zinnia and a dozen purple pansies in their backyard garden. Brant had planted the flowers. Hem Raj had surprised them with the statue, stating, quietly and with deep reverence, that Parvati was the deity of love, harmony and marriage.

It had been six weeks since their return from Agra.

Sitting now at their sleek new glass patio table, under a soft afternoon sun, Lloyd still in his slippers reading, Brant took comfort in the fact that the goddess was watching over their union.

"We're meeting Pat and Benny tonight, yes?" Lloyd said, flipping a page of the magazine he was reading. "Or was that later this week?"

"Tonight," Brant said. "You know something…"

Lloyd turned to him. They were sitting close, in a set of striped canvas patio chairs that Brant had bought the week prior. Lloyd took his hand, lifted it to his mouth, and kissed it. It was a new habit of his.

"I don't know if Hem Raj has children," Brant said.

Lloyd turned back to his magazine. A green canary lighted on Parvati's stone head.

"A daughter in college and a younger son," Lloyd said.

Brant pulled his naked legs up under him, settling

in the chair. He wore a green silk robe with nothing on underneath. They'd made love that morning and he didn't want to shower yet, holding onto his husband's scent.

He wanted to ask more about Hem Raj but felt vaguely ashamed realizing that he knew so little about a man he saw every day, a man who had seem him through a very rough patch. He'd overheard Hem Raj on the telephone the day before, speaking in Hindi. The tone of his voice was unmistakably kind, loving. He first imagined a secret affair. Then he recalled Lloyd mentioning something about a wife or brother.

The brilliant green canary rose a foot, then settled back on Parvati's smooth head.

"We're going to that place at the Oberoi hotel. Tasting menu. You'll like it," Lloyd said.

"It will be a gas," Brant said.

"What?"

Brant laughed quietly. He'd started repeating phrases he read in Carol's journal. Lloyd stood up and stretched. His movement sent the canary skyward. A gentle breeze blew.

"Summer's almost done. Now we move into the most beautiful season," Lloyd said softly. "And the celebration of Diwali."

He turned and smiled happily at Brant, and this struck Brant deeply, sadness and joy merging because indeed after a very stormy start, things were moving beautifully for the two of them. He watched Parvati, hoping she would smile in recognition, but of course, she was only stone.

Chapter 22

Mendah's driver took her and Brant to her favorite luncheon spot in the Santushti shopping complex, a gated oasis off a torn-up two-lane.

"Come on! You know her, that actress. Tall blonde I know, aren't they all blonde, but she was in that film about a lobster. Everybody loved it," she said, lighting a cigarette in the car, then touching the driver's shoulder and speaking in Hindi. "Ham do ghanta rahenge."

The car pulled over and the pair stepped out onto the ragged street. On one side was an abandoned lot. In front of the lot lay several overturned ancient wooden carts. A heavy-set shirtless man sat precariously on one of the carts, watching them. On the other side of the road were tall silver gates leading into Santushti. There was a chunk of the road missing just ahead. Mendah knelt by a hole with grace, despite her formidable girth, immense bust and very high heels. She waved Brant over.

"This looks like a star," she said. "Like they carved out a star."

Brant approached with no intention of getting down for a closer look. Mendah stood and took his hand.

"Don't you dare tell me it's a sign," she said, dragging her cigarette then stubbing it with the point of her heel. "But it is very odd."

Brant laughed as she guided him through the silver

73

gates into the elegant plaza. This was only their second meeting, but they'd become fast friends.

"That very same actress came to Delhi for a film shoot and left with Marla's husband but then Marla got even." Mendah said. "Remind me to tell you about the icepick."

The plaza was circular, a pale stone path leading around a series of boutiques whose double glass doorways revealed glimpses of silk dresses, things in pink bottles and shoes with feathers. At the end of the path was the Diggin Café.

In front of the café at a skinny podium stood a young Indian woman with lacquered black hair. She wore a bird's-eye blue silk smock. She kissed Mendah's cheek and led them past a waiting trio into a small main room. A black bar was manned by a striking fellow rotating a martini shaker. Brant noticed his manicured haircut, the sides shaved to the skin topped with a deep brown lushness.

The hostess guided them out onto a small platform overlooking a garden where diners chattered. There were several large flowering trees lining the perimeter of the cloistered spot which gave the entire garden a sense of being shrouded in pink. On the platform was a single wrought iron table. Brant noticed the backs of the chairs were carved to look like vines. Mendah sat at the platform table and breathlessly finished her story.

"He left the actress after six months in Los Angeles and came back to Marla. Though I use the term actress very broadly. She's on a housewife show now so you tell me." Mendah said. "I still think my nose is too big. I've always thought that. Such a bother."

During their first meeting for drinks, which turned

into a riotous five-hour escapade, Brant discovered that Mendah's thoughts were of the hummingbird type. It was useless to try to follow too closely or question her. She had no capacity to go backwards. She was furiously driven by an inner sense of discovering.

He'd so far pieced together that Mendah spent a large chunk of her life in Manhattan before settling in Delhi five years ago with her second husband, Omar, a mega-wealthy "rug salesman of sorts" as she described him.

Mendah leaned on the platform's delicate iron railing observing. Her green silk pant suit cinched and flowed at all the right spots. One bold white stripe cut down the center of her shoulder length black hair. Brant guessed she was forty. While she shared similarities with the Indian women just below, sumptuous silks draped over shoulders, shimmering jewels, studied grace, her style was a touch more direct, bordering on a delightfully bold and careless arrogance.

"They all hated me. Like being a whore is such a terrible thing," she said, turning back to Brant. "But that was before Omar did business with their husbands. He's richer than, well…Did you bring Carol?"

Brant had mentioned the journal and she'd insisted he bring it to lunch. The bartender with the asymmetrical hair approached.

"He's really the best dish here," she said to Brant, then to the man. "Let's do coconut martinis. And bring us the lunch menu."

Brant was not a day drinker, but in Mendah's orbit he felt a new daring.

"I promise you these martinis rival those at Il Divo in

Manhattan. I want you to read Carol to me."

"Now?" Brant said.

"Not all of it, just a taste."

Brant had the journal in a small leather satchel that hung over his shoulder like a purse. He hesitated, feeling protective of Carol's life, a past scribbled in rushed bits revealing what thrilled or disturbed her to such an extent that she had to get it down. As he drew it out slowly, there was a rising shame, broken by the closeness of the returning waiter and the bright timbre of Mendah's voice.

"I'm so glad you're here today, the weekend waiter is a bore," Mendah said, all her attention on the attractive young man who deposited the drinks. "Give us a bit of time with these."

Brant lifted the delicate coupe glass to his mouth, noticing clusters of women sipping similar concoctions, imagining this was a glass Carol would lift, maybe at this very spot. And here he was, a man yes, but more so, just another housewife really. A shimmering thing. He set down his drink and opened the journal.

"From the top?" he said.

"Oh no, I always start a book in the middle or just read the end. Pick a random spot," Mendah said.

Brant paused. He'd been methodical in his slow discovering. Mendah was staring so he opened the journal to the center and scanned a page, noticing the word lunch. Clearly a sign. He read softly at first, finding his voice.

"*The strangest thing happened. I was out for lunch with Miriam. She's a beast. Loves the heat and insists we eat al fresco. I sometimes wonder if she's truly human, or some otherling. She never ceases to amaze me, smoking through lunch, nibbling, us alone in that little restaurant which was lovely despite it being so damn hot. I did eat less. Maybe that's her trick for staying thin."*

Mendah gasped and lifted her bejeweled hand.

"This is 1945? She sounds so modern. I imagined; oh I don't know. Something stuffy."

The waiter appeared.

"Can you handle one more of these drinks?" Mendah said. "And why don't we do avocado toast. Is that all right or am I being impossibly bossy?"

Brant nodded in assent. He'd been drawn quickly into Carol's world, a swift and deep connection that felt natural when he was alone, but a bit unnerving in public.

"Read a little more," Mendah said. "Then I have some gossip."

Brant turned back to Carol.

"I noticed him watching me, just outside the restaurant's entrance which was flagged by two large flowering bushes. He was just off center, holding a newspaper and wearing a striped suit. He had on a hat. I noticed, because we were the only two there, he was alone and clearly staring. I do get the dead eye glare a lot, but mostly from the locals because I'm an American woman. This man was extremely pale, ghostly really. Tall with very long arms."

"Spooky!" Mendah said loudly, startling Brant. "No wonder you're obsessed with this woman. I want to borrow it when you're done. But first…"

A stately woman with snow white hair wearing a soft pink sari passed their table, nodding at Mendah. Once she passed, Mendah began.

"You'd never guess right?"

"Guess what?" Brant said.

Mendah sipped her drink.

"Her, with the white hair. Regal right? She snubbed me until I ran into her at a bar. She was with a younger man. Not her husband. Did I finish telling you the ice pick story?" she said.

The waiter arrived with two plates of avocado toast.

"This you are going to love. They add a touch of saffron. I wasn't aware how hungry I was, now taste it and tell me the truth," Mendah said, snapping open her pink napkin.

Brant, already dizzy from the drink, hesitated, not knowing if he was meant to pick it up or cut into it. Mendah was slicing, so he did the same. He wanted to hear the end of her story, but he imagined it had drifted off to the ethereal resting spot where all her half-told bits landed.

He made a note to reach out to Jasmine, and thank him for the connection. Mendah was the bright distraction he absolutely needed.

Chapter 23

Hem Raj picked Brant up at the restaurant after lunch.

During the long slow ride home through tremendous traffic, he became increasingly anxious. Trapped in the stuffy vehicle, windows tightly shut against blaring horns and beggars, he struggled to catch his breath. He was bothered by the fact that he'd skipped ahead in the journal and shared it with Mendah. He had carelessly obliterated a part of Carol's life and broken a trust, reading aloud what was once so private.

He needed to go back to where he'd left off the day before. He had the journal in his bag, but he could not read in the car. It gave him a terrible headache. He had to wait to get home to rectify his mistake.

It was nearly an hour before they arrived. He hurried into the kitchen, then onto the back patio armed with a tall gin and tonic. Thank God Lloyd worked late. He quickly found his place:

Gerald is in the other room. I can hear him puttering about. This is risky but I can stuff you under my pillow if he comes into the bedroom. I can hear him whistling.

He gave me a compliment today, said how nice my hair looks and I ran into the bathroom and cried. He really is a good man. I couldn't let him see me fall apart. He's bound to figure it out if I don't watch it. I'm not an emotional girl. He always says that. "You're tough as a man Carol." He'll know something's up if I fall apart.

The fact is I'm a real goner. I'm leading a double life. Each time I see Ajan, I tell myself it's the last. Then he does things, says things. And I fall even harder. How long can I get away with this?

In the margin, a scribbled note. Is G mother coming. Buy him a special birthday gift. Cuff links?

I'm all jelly inside. Just like one of those fish on the shore. Was it only two summers ago. On the shore with Gerald, Nancy, Bob. Screaming about a jellyfish.

The last time. We were naked in another ratty hotel room. Ajan put his lips to my ear. But he didn't take them away. He kept his mouth there, using his tongue, whispering in his language. Nibbling. It was the most wonderful…

There was a jarring scratch across the page.

Brant shut the journal. He heard Lloyd come in the front door. He'd come out to the patio soon. They'd have another drink. Brant finished his gin and tonic and felt a rushing urge to hide the journal. But these were not his secrets, not his transgression. That was paid for, penance done. Still, he shared a quiet shame with Carol. A trembling bit of darkness he did not want in the light.

He imagined Gerald had walked in on Carol. That's why she scratched the pen across the page. In panic. Had he seen what she was writing? Had he figured it all out?

Lloyd called from the living room.

"Yes, another drink," Brant answered, shutting the journal tightly and covering it with a magazine from the table. "Yes, come and join me."

Chapter 24

The slick sweat covering every inch of their bodies created such an intense gliding rhythm during Brant's starry moment that he nearly lost consciousness. He shouted in bed, arching, there were colors, and collapsing he began to laugh, wondering how at his age he was still able to have one of his mind-altering orgasms, something he'd long ago tucked away as belonging to his wild teen years. Yet, here it was, re-emerging. And settling down against the pillow in that sex-dew twilight, he thought of Carol in his bedside table drawer.

Lloyd was gasping, still breathing very heavily. He rolled onto his side and spoke but Brant couldn't hear him. It was after midnight. Night starlings were singing.

Brant sat up slowly. He was still reeling and couldn't piece himself fully together.

"Are those birds singing outside?" Brant said.

Lloyd turned to face Brant, pulling him close and kissing him.

"You were a fiercesome little tiger. I thought you might start howling."

They lay together, listening to the Indian night. Brant had momentarily thought of Carol's randy lover Ajan during sex. It must have been when Lloyd licked inside his ear, the way Ajan had for Carol. He stifled an urge to reach for the journal, to write Carol a giddy note about what they shared, for the pages surely held magic, connecting him to her spirit, a past not forgotten.

Brant rolled away from his husband, still quaking with pleasure.

"Hey," Lloyd said sleepily. "I would love an omelet."

Brant took up his blue silk robe from the end of the bed and went to the window facing the yard. It was too hot, and too late to eat. Lloyd often demanded food after sex, but it passed quickly. He would soon fall asleep. He was like that. It was part of their routine. Brant would pretend to go make the food. But it would never happen.

He could still hear the singing of the strange night birds. Far off, the traffic's constant hum. He thought of Ajan – dark, naked, lean and perhaps violent. Did he demand things of Carol?

With the bird calls fading came Lloyd's soft snoring. Brant smiled. He liked his husband's predictability. Then Lloyd began to mumble in his sleep. Brant turned and moved closer to the bed. Lloyd was on his back. He was smiling. Both of his arms were over his head. Brant leaned in to kiss his forehead but paused. Lloyd moaned softly. He seemed to have moved so quickly into a dream-state.

"Dirt," he said softly, almost like a purring. "Take that off…oh…Samir."

Abruptly, Lloyd turned on his side and went silent.

Brant walked slowly to his side of the bed and got in. He lay still. He was very tired but was disturbed by what his husband said, not just the words, but the soft and sensual tone of it. There was too much in it, he thought. There was something there he did not like or fully understand. Though too, there was something hauntingly familiar.

Chapter 25

"She isn't as she appears, know that."

Brant leaned close to his laptop taking in a lush tableau. Jasmine rested on a gigantic frosty pink pillow in front of a floor to ceiling picture window. Behind him the French Alps rose a muted blue against pearly clouds.

"I like her," Brant said of Mendah. "How did you two meet?"

His head wrapped in a cream turban, wearing a red silk robe, Jasmine smiled coquettishly.

"Let's just say we ran in the same circles for a while," he said. "Tell me about Carol. You said there's a problem?"

Brant was in the backyard, facing the garden. Lloyd was inside making lunch. The light behind Jasmine vanished, a rack of clouds swallowing the sun. For a moment he appeared as an outline, a figure made of shadows.

Brant heard the sliding door into the living room open behind him.

"Who is that?" Lloyd said.

Brant turned.

"Jasmine, on Skype. He's in Geneva."

Lloyd waved, turning to go back in.

"Hey Jasmine," he said. Then to Brant, "Lunch is ready but no rush."

When Brant returned his focus to the screen, Jasmine was again fully lit.

"I worry about you alone, so far away," Brant said.

"This from someone running around Delhi," Jasmine said. "I'm fine. Really. He's a gentle little bear. A software engineer back in the States. Now tell me about Carol."

"I've been thinking," Brant said.

"Uh oh," Jasmine said playfully.

Brant turned, witnessing Lloyd through the glass doors, moving across the room.

"I'm afraid," Brant began. "Maybe I should let go of Carol. Bury her back there where I found her. Before it starts to infect me."

"That's a bit dramatic," Jasmine said. "Do you see yourself in her?"

Brant paused, considering.

"We both made mistakes. But I think she's headed toward something dangerous."

Pulling her robe close to her neck, Jasmine turned thoughtfully toward the view of the Alps, then back to the screen.

"Remember what I told you?"

"About threes?"

There was the chiming of a clock, but it was an odd, high-pitched shimmering sound, almost like a wind chime.

"You need to complete Carol's journey. She has things to teach you. It's part of your discovery, I'm certain of that," Jasmine said. "You are going to be all right. Trust the process."

The clock stopped chiming. A man's voice called softly but Brant could not make out the words.

"Is that him?" Brant said.

"A bientot," Jasmine called back, then softer. "I have to go. You might meet this one when we're back in New York. Promise me you will finish your reading. They are just words on a page, remember. It has something very important to give you. And honey, you are not Carol."

Brant still had a hundred questions, but he nodded in acquiescence. As the shadow of what he presumed was a man this time fell across Jasmine, his friend blew a kiss and disappeared from screen.

Chapter 26

Shortly after dawn Brant woke, stumbled from bed and rushed out to the patio gasping for air. It was as if the house had sunk deep into the ancient Indian earth burying him. He could not breathe. Only as his feet felt the grass, only as he saw the garden, did he draw a deep ragged breath, clawing at his throat to make sure he was not being strangled by an unseen force.

He had dreamt of Carol, something he had never done. She was with a man, who was Ajan, then in the dream became Samir though nothing changed in his appearance. Carol and the man were having sex, then were on a boat and, as he woke, Carol was being thrown into black murky water.

He touched his throat again. His breathing was returning to normal. He would need to read more to find a relief. Maybe that's what Jasmine meant. He would finish Carol's story and understand *her* brief season in Delhi.

Standing, he stretched then went back inside for the journal. Lloyd would sleep late. He settled back in the yard with coffee and Carol.

Over two weeks with no word from Ajan. I know it's a hidden blessing. He is no good. A cad. He could ruin my life with Gerald. Still. Each day I feel a bit more desperate. He can't just disappear. It can't be over forever. I told Miriam I had to see him and she warned me. Said things had changed, that she

87

didn't seen any of the regular fellows. Something was off, she kept saying, applying her lipstick, shaking up a drink, let it go. It's over.

Of course, I couldn't. I've been searching. The bar, that ratty hotel. Then finally at the diplomat's club last night, in the ladies' room, the pair of us in our mirrors fussing, she said to me as the powder room emptied out. She spoke in a raspy whisper. He's in jail. I knew what she meant still I said. Who? She turned on the faucet then turned to me. Don't be an idiot. Ajan. He's locked up. We shouldn't even say his name. I said to her, I will go see him.

I said it without thinking, as if my lips moved though I was no longer there. She slapped me. She slapped me hard. It left a mark. She's caught up in something too I thought.

Brant shut the journal. He thought of locking it away. Like candy in a drawer. Liquor in a cabinet. He felt more and more protective of her telling. He would not share it with anyone from this point on. But as Jasmine said, he would finish it. He had to see this through. There was no turning back.

Chapter 27

Brant woke and hanging in that ethereal moment between disintegrating dream and truth, he imagined Carol lying asleep on the bed next to him filling the curved outline Lloyd had left. He reached for Carol in the bedside table with startling urgency but then seeing the clock, set her aside. He'd overslept and was late for a meeting with Mendah. He did not want to rush his Carol time. He'd take the journal along.

They were having tea on the third-floor patio of a lavish little luncheon spot. He'd managed to somehow arrive a touch early. Mendah was due soon. The table, one of three on the long narrow overhang, was situated very close to the railing, looking out onto the seething street below. Hovering there, lifting his hand-painted china cup, Brant felt a pang of guilt over the outrageous contrast. Small flat-bed trucks and carts crowded with men sped past honking, a never-ending swarm of people darting in and out of small shops with dingy striped awnings. A pair of emaciated cows slumbered. A child swatted flies furiously, laughing.

He opened Carol.

Dearest journal, should I just burn you like the dress. Bury you or tear you up. Things are all right now. But –

In the margin. *More sleep powder from Dr. Hangar. G may not like it. Hide that too?*

I need to sleep straight through one night. I escaped scandal.

Yes. That's what matters, I told Miriam that yesterday. She laughed, but it was a dark laugh, bitter. It could have all gone so sideways. But I burned that dress. I want to burn the whole summer. Could I ever have done all that? No matter. Miriam's right. Move on. Don't look back. Ajan is locked away. I dated a convict. I'll take that to the grave! I think they keep them away for a long time here. I guess that makes me safe. I should have seen it coming that's what Miriam said and yes she's right. I thought I was so smart.

I still think of him. If he showed up. If he got out. I'd go to him. Thank heavens that's not going to happen. It scares the living daylights out of me.

I don't think Gerald suspects a thing. Poor dope. Miriam says "You need to get your hems straight. Lay low." I'm damn lucky to have gotten through it with my skin.

There is a sharp line nearly like a stab across the page.

Gerald is early. Need a better hiding place for this. How do you act normal when your mind is all to pieces?

"Back to the *Carol* woman," Mendah said slipping onto the small balcony.

A waiter followed her with a silver chalice of coffee and a plate of sweets.

"How's your *living* husband?" Mendah said.

Brant laughed out loud. He enjoyed Mendah's dry humor, her hard line on things.

"Working a lot."

"Well," Mendah said, accepting a small plate of cookies from the waiter. "How's the Diwali party planning?"

She lifted a cookie to taste.

Brant looked out at the strange, busy street. A few

months ago he never would have imagined any of this – Delhi, Mendah, Carol, those cows.

"There is something with Lloyd," he began. "He was dreaming, and I heard him mention someone."

"What?"

"Samir. He said Samir. That's a man's name right?"

"Sure, it can be."

Brant sighed loudly.

"He sounded excited. We don't know anyone named Samir."

Mendah ate another cookie. The cows lowed in the distance.

"You had a dalliance in Sugar Springs yes?"

"Cold Springs."

"So worst case, he had a fling with Samir. Isn't that part of the setup? Tit for tat. I mean, what is it that's under your skin?"

"Oh, I don't know," Brant said softly. "And no we don't have an agreement like that."

Suddenly Mendah stood up, turned and leaned on the thin railing. She wore a golden silk pant suit, belted, and the thick green multi-patterned band in her black hair matched the pattern on her wedge-heeled shoes. Brant marveled at her silhouette there, as if it were pasted against the relentlessly blue sky, that searing sun, the blur grayed chaos of the street below.

"Come here," she said, not turning. "Look at him. He's not worried."

Brant stood up and joined her at the rail. The boy swatting the flies turned as if on cue and waved. "Ask Lloyd about it. It's likely nothing."

Brant felt an urge to put his arm around her shoulder but stifled it. Mendah lifted her hand, waving to the child. He ran across the street and began dancing a frantic oddly lascivious jig. Mendah clapped.

"Should I throw money?" Brant asked.

Mendah clapped more loudly then turned back and sat.

"You are such an American princess," she said. "Is it late enough to order a drink?"

Brant studied the child below. He was sure he should throw something down. The boy stopped dancing, then began to wave both hands in the air. A cart, pulled by an ancient-looking donkey, crept past behind the boy, and someone began to yell in Hindi. The boy ran away. He imagined his fear about Lloyd, the sense that he'd heard something wicked he should not have heard, was running off with the boy. Mendah was right. He worried far too much.

Brant turned back to Mendah, deciding it was indeed time for a drink.

"Let's plan my Diwali party," he said.

Chapter 28

Brant told Hem Raj his plan to host a Diwali party as they weeded the backyard garden under the morning shadow of Parvati. Hem Raj glanced at the stone goddess hovering, surrounded by marigolds. He abruptly stopped and sat quietly for several moments, then said:

"You know, that is a very special time."

Brant paused, wiping sweat from his brow. He sensed a gentle judgment.

"Would this be," Brant paused, thinking. "Disrespectful?"

Hem Raj smiled, removing his green gardening gloves then sitting back on his haunches in the early morning sunlight, giving Brant his full attention.

"Do not misunderstand me. It is a beautiful idea. Diwali celebrates the triumph of light over darkness and good over evil," he said. "It is simply that I have obligations and will not be able to work or assist. But I can bring in others to help."

Hem Raj glanced over Brant's shoulder.

"He is awake."

Lloyd sleepily stepped out into the yard and as Brant turned, he watched him move barefoot across the lawn. He wore his emerald green silk pajamas which moved and shimmered in the now bright morning sun. His hair was askew, and he stumbled a step as he approached, then he held out a hand to Brant who was on his knees near Hem Raj. Brant took Lloyd's hand and without warning they were dancing, Lloyd guiding and pulling him close moving in a haphazard waltz then a clumsy two-step. Brant laughed with surprise and self-consciousness that Hem Raj was watching. He leaned into his husband, his cheek on silk and shut his eyes as Lloyd swayed with him across the hot morning lawn. As they traveled, as his feet moved so easily and his body felt so light, Brant wondered if they might stay in Delhi longer than the six months, might even settle, put down roots, something he had never to this very moment even considered. But bright brushes against things so happy had a way of doing that, he knew, and too he realized these tiny bursts of realization happened almost exclusively when he was holding Lloyd.

Chapter 29

Very late, unable to sleep and increasingly nervous about the upcoming Diwali party, Brant went to the back patio. At first a bright little lark, the event had morphed into a monstrous thing, a glaring reflection on Brant's incapacity as a host and perhaps, as a husband.

Lloyd had let him know, on several occasions, that the evening had become increasingly important, a perfect testament of how he as an American had integrated with the Delhi team. All the "most important" people were coming, Lloyd shared with glee.

Brant shrank with each declaration, alarmingly aware of his complete ineptitude at party planning. Mendah, fortunately, had stepped in to help. Still, the pressure felt enormous.

Sitting alone under the sweeping black night sky, he took up Carol. He wanted to finish the entire story before the party. He felt by completing something he had taken into his heart, a journey of a flawed woman he had grown to identify with, that he might feel some scrap of accomplishment.

Picking up the journal, he found his place and began. He'd caught up to the part that he'd shared with Mendah during their lunch. Carol had discovered the man in the striped suit.

The strangest thing happened. I was out for lunch with

Miriam.

I noticed him watching me, just outside the restaurant's entrance which was flagged by two large flowering bushes. He was just off center, holding a newspaper and wearing a striped suit. He had on a hat. I noticed, because we were the only two there, he was alone and clearly staring. I do get the dead eye glare a lot, but mostly from the locals because I'm an American woman.

This man was extremely pale, ghostly really. Tall with very long arms. They hung limply at his sides, one hand holding the folded newspaper, as if he were waiting for a bus. He saw me seeing him and he did not look away and I said something to Miriam. "Not my type," was all she said, with that unflappable confidence of hers, the sense that all men want her. She's a corker. I'll give her that. But what happened next is what has me shaken.

I'd forgotten him and was arguing with Miriam about who was better at tennis. I saw her look up then I looked up and there he was. Standing just a foot from our table.

"May I speak with you," he said.

I knew he was addressing me. His voice was soft, but cold in a threatening way. He frightened me and I did not know why. After all the mess with Ajan I spook easily.

"Scram," Miriam said, lighting another cigarette.

"It's important. Can you step over here," he said, just as softly.

I don't know why, but I got up and followed him toward the gate where the flowering bushes stood. I had a terrible premonition that if I did not, he would find me another time, and I might be alone. I made sure to stay in clear view of

Miriam. I turned and faced her, so his back was to her and I could see her.

At once, he seemed to relax. He smiled, and his teeth were as white as his powdery skin. He reached into his suit coat pocket, pulled out a cigarette and put it in his mouth, all the while holding onto the newspaper. He pulled out a match, lit the cigarette, exhaled, then smiled again.

"I won't keep you," he said, drawing on the cigarette. "It's very simple. It's about Ajan."

I instinctively stepped backwards at the mention of his name, nearly bumping into the bush. This made the strange man laugh, then pull a bit of tobacco off his tongue, still smiling broadly. Miriam, who had been watching all along, stood up.

"He's left you in charge of a certain debt," he said. "Unfortunate, but that's that."

Miriam moved toward us.

"I don't understand," I said.

"I don't think you want to involve your pretty friend. Meet me at 7 tonight."

He took my hand and quickly pushed a slip of paper into it. As Miriam reached us, he turned, as if he expected her, tipped his hat, and left.

"What the hell?" she said.

The scene ended abruptly and Brant turned the page to find it blank. In a panic, he turned several more blank pages, then found her there. The ink had gone from black to blue.

"Miriam – this next bit is for you. But then my dear - maybe all of this is. Who else would read my scribbles? I will tell you where I hide this just in case.

The fact is things went a bit murky after I saw the man in

the striped suit. I know! You forbade me to see him - the strange man in the striped suit as we called him that day at lunch. Meet me at 7, he said. Absolutely not you said. You are so bossy! Honestly, I imagined he was going to tell me that Ajan wanted me to take him cigarettes or something in prison. A conjugal visit. Something harmless like that. I know you said forget all about Ajan. But…I can't, at least not completely. I suppose I will always love Ajan in a way. I think of him. Lusty dreams. I wake and smell him as if he just touched me and only left a moment ago. That scent of patchouli and strong cigarettes. It stained me. All right, I see you now laughing out loud at my purple prose.

But I feel a secret gratitude, an affection I suppose. Which is why I felt so drawn to the man in the striped suit. A little obsessed. I had to see him, to see it all through you know? To end it all or so I thought.

Brant quickly turned the page. Carol had jotted a short list which seemed odd in the midst of her confession to Miriam. He looked up and he could swear the swarm of stars above were trembling in anticipation. He considered getting a cocktail but thought better of it.

He honestly imagined she'd written it all in one long rush. But perhaps in stages. Like his reading of it, like his experience with her.

Pick up fabric for blouse, more gin.

And then:

"Miriam I was going to tell you in person, but things have gone so oddly sideways. I am not so much afraid, but it's just very strange. And I feel getting this all down in ink (or this stubby pencil!) is best. So, here we go dearest.

I thought of asking you to go with me, to meet him (our striped suit man), but knew you'd talk me out of it.

We met in Old Delhi, one of those terrible little stone side streets in the middle of it all. There were so many people, all the animals you know. I thought what could be more safe? Yet, when I sat down dear, I felt just swallowed up. There was so much going on, the tiny table in front of the tiny store front where he sat waiting, a brass carafe of that terrible coffee and two cups on the table already. I realized that because there was so so much going on, he could likely do anything, say anything with very little notice. Still, I sat down, determined.

Aren't I brave – I know you are rolling your eyes, saying no you are simply foolish.

Brant took a deep breath, speaking in a whisper, glancing out at the burial spot where he'd discovered Carol. "Yes you are brave Carol," he said to the night before continuing his reading. "You are not foolish."

He started right in. Looked right at me as if he was in the middle of a sentence. It was noisy – shops, people, animals all of it. A man with an eye patch was watching us from the doorway of the coffee stand. To the right and left were a spice shop and a fruit spot. So much haggling and yelling yet I heard him, the man in the striped suit, as if his lips were next to my ear. He was Indian and spoke very distinctly.

"You American women should be more careful," was how he started. I was wearing a white dress, the one with the tulips on the sleeves and I thought how odd I must look, sitting in all of this muck. "Your lover has set you up in a situation."

I stopped him. "He is not my lover."

He ignored me.

"The details don't matter," he said. Or something like that. He spoke quickly. This is how I remember it anyway.

"You have a debt to pay. It is not negotiable. It will only take one night. Then you will be done. There is a man you will meet. It won't take long. We will take over once he asks you to leave with him. You will tell him you know where the money is hidden..."

An ox cart rattled by two men shouting. Dust blew into our tiny cups of coffee and onto my white dress. The man in the striped suit stood up. He handed me a slip of paper.

"Be here on the 15th of this month. And the second address at the bottom, that is what you will share."

He bowed. Then before he went, he bent closer and said the worst part, the part really that made me write all this down. And this I remember exactly as he said it:

"If you do not come, the consequences will be dire."

The pen trailed off. Brant shut the journal, feeling a chill despite the heat. He had read it all so quickly. Was it coming so fast to an end? It was still the middle of the night and he knew he should go to bed but he could not sleep now. He had to finish.

Brant ran his hand along the page with a sort of blessing. He didn't want her to be harmed. He wondered if she would be. Only a few handwritten pages left. Is that the end of dear Carol?

"Miriam you must embrace the role of confidante. I know that sounds so serious, but that's that. I must get the rest down, quickly, before I forget. I will give it to you, and you will read it.

I went on the 15th. I took a rickshaw several blocks from the named hotel, my first mistake. Well, my second, as I should

100

have taken you with me. I should have told you of all of this. But I was convinced and maybe still am, I don't know – that I am embroiled in a dirty little detective novel, something Graham Greene would cook up, that I need to see to the bitter end my dear. For Ajan's sake. So, I went.

I got out of the rickshaw at the edge of the marketplace, by that spice market we go to. It was so hot, but then it's always so hot. There were too many people, more than normal. Throngs and throngs coming at me, as if they were all headed toward me and I was the only person going deeper into the terrible cobblestone street, deeper toward the chaotic store fronts, toward the hotel at the other end of the block. Even the animals were coming at me, those sad thin cows and horrible dogs. But I was steely, dear, so strong I thought.

I marched forward in my red mules, my white dress, hair tied up with a flowered scarf looking like God knows what to these people, men and boys hauling carts and shouting, so much shouting and children running in circles, brushing past me as I marched on, staring up at me, yanking on my dress holding out their hands for money from the pretty white woman. But on I marched, I didn't dare open my purse to offer them a rupee.

Halfway down the street, halted momentarily by a donkey passing, I stopped and in the pause I was swept with a sudden terror. I was the only woman and was in the center of a madness, surrounded on all sides. The sound was deafening as I stood terribly still, like a stone in a fast-rushing river. They all just flowed quickly and effortlessly around me. The stores on either side had so many people dipping into giant bushels of red and brown spices, grabbing strands of hanging beads and ahead were feathers flying, chickens being haggled over.

I could see the hotel rising two stories at the end of the street. I should have turned back, I see you shaking your head now Miriam, but I did not.

I was halfway there and I thought I've got to get this done, to finish this. I am a determined girl Miriam, you know that. So on I went.

I began walking quickly and I felt better. I looked straight ahead to avoid all the staring eyes. The hotel was coming closer to me, that's how it felt, not like I was moving against the tide, like it was coming to me. I was very thirsty by the time I reached the place.

The instructions had been clear. Go to the second floor to room 206. Don't knock, simply enter. Don't wait for anyone to open the door. I wondered if the hotel had a bar, a glass of something cool might steady my nerves. But looking up, I noticed there were tiny balconies fronting the second-floor rooms. There were only four rooms across the front, and at one of them, a curtain opened. I could not see who was there, due to the intensity of the mid-day sun, but I was sure someone was watching me. I mounted the short, battered staircase up to the entrance and stepped in.

Inside, the place was shabby. The type, if we stepped into Miriam, we'd dash away laughing. A rusty ceiling fan, rattan lobby furniture that looked as if it had been soaked in the rain and chewed by rats.

The first thing that told me to turn heel and run (again, yes again Miriam) was the lack of anyone there. The front desk, as it were – really nothing but a dirty wooden counter – was empty. Not a soul. There was a wide staircase at the end of the square lobby, shooting up to the second floor. It was at this point

102

I thought seriously of going back to get you Miriam, and I felt not afraid but foolish. This couldn't be real. It was all a ruse, Ajan teasing me from his cell, setting me up for a ridiculous fright. Twisting his knife of resentment, a little sharper, he stuck behind bars, me free.

I nearly turned away but then I heard a clock. It struck the hour and I realized I was late. The sense of time rushing past, of the moment going, frightened me and I mounted the stairs to face my fate.

Step by step, images rushed ahead of me. A man behind the door, terrors, nothing at all, even you Miriam. And finally, as I stood at 206, Ajan himself, taunting me because God knows I still want him, how ashamed I am of that little detail.

I went in. I will tell you of the man that I saw, and what occurred, and you will tell me what to do next. How to reckon with this mess!

What shocked me most, as I stepped into the room, was how elegant he appeared. A tall, thin older man, near sixty I think, wearing a crisp white linen suit, with a full head of silver hair, smoking a long cigarette, poised in a rattan chair. The room was like the lobby. A derelict bed, dirty bedding, one window with gray curtains pushed to the side revealing the chaos of the street below. An ash can. But amidst it, like a strange white lotus, sat the man I was told to meet.

"I will not ask you to sit my dear. I apologize for this place. It's disgusting. I will be brief."

At that he dropped his cigarette onto the floor and squashed it with the toe of his long black leather shoe. I recall that move because his shoes were shined to a spit. I took a step back as he took a step forward. He smiled. I knew my line, the words I was meant to say. But he continued before I could draw a breath.

"Am I that terrible?" he said.

He took a light step forward and I stayed still. I noticed (and yes this is a detail for you Miriam, you know just in case!) I noticed his eyebrows were very thin and dark, not like his silver hair. They appeared to be drawn on, which I found so strange.

"Your lover is relying on you," he began, taking one more step forward. "To be clear, his life depends on you."

I can hear that phrase still, though the rest of what he said, after revealing that, is a bit garbled in my memory. He spoke to me like a child he was explaining a lesson to, about a task that had to be done. The trouble is, I believe what he said. And I think if I do not do what he told me to do, Ajan will vanish. That's what he said, "Vanish." He said that word vanish, so softly, with a slight smile, as he sat back down, moved away from me and lit another cigarette, so quietly and simply but with such finality. I knew it was true. I will tell you the rest in person. It was all too horrible and I can't bear to write it here, it happened so quickly. But at least I got this much down, so if I were to "vanish" I pray you find this."

And that was it.

The journal had at least another twenty pages, but they were blank. Brant shut the book, turned away from the dark night and went into bed exhausted and deeply unsatisfied. He felt as if he'd been cheated on, pushed violently away and shut out from whatever was the real end, be it cruel or glorious, of his Carol.

Part 4

Chapter 30

Through the glass doorway into the living room Brant glimpsed Lloyd embracing a young man. He and Mendah were standing near the garden where he'd dug up Carol. He turned to Mendah as a trio of sharp blasts rang in the distance. Fireworks exploded. A heavy haze hung low.

"Happy Diwali! That will go on all night," Mendah said, taking Brant's arm. "The air quality is terrible. We should really be inside but it's getting crowded in there. How many do you expect?"

Brant considered mentioning what he'd witnessed but decided against it. He had to stay on point.

"Twenty or thirty. All from Lloyd's company. You're my only guest," Brant said, smiling weakly. "There are a few of the men's wives inside. I should talk to them but I'd rather stay with you. I'm a wretched host."

There was an eruption of voices, then loud laughter as a small group of men entered the lawn from the house, high ball glasses in hand. They wore colorful hats, something Lloyd had come up with. There was a high-pitched whistle, and far off, the evening sky appeared momentarily red.

"Brant!"

It was Lloyd calling. Mendah took his arm, guiding him away from the back garden toward the men.

"Your husband needs you dearest," she said. "You're doing just fine."

The cluster, several Americans and one Indian, watched them approach. Strands of yellow fairy lights, hung around the edges of the house, came slowly to life as dusk set in.

The men formed a semi-circle, Brant and Mendah joining them to close the gap. Lloyd made introductions. They were all his colleagues. There was Billings, a squat forty-something fellow who was sweating profusely and guzzling his drink; John, lean, frail, older with a sour look; to Benny, the youngest and most attractive with a hive of wavy black hair and big biceps; and finally Samir, the one young Indian man in the group.

Brant hesitated before taking Samir's hand. He knew it was the man his husband had dreamed about, something he'd never addressed. He was also likely the man he'd seen Lloyd hug through the glass doorway.

Samir had a long narrow face, a pointed nose, and large seeking eyes. He appeared to be about thirty, was physically fit in a lean tennis player way and wore a traditional Indian smock tucked into white cotton trousers. A turquoise necklace hugged his neck. Mendah gave Brant a quick glance, her eyes brightening with mischief at the mention of his name.

"It's wonderful of you to celebrate our holiday," Samir said, with a short bow.

His voice was very deep, his words weighted with sincerity. It was not what Brant expected. He looked toward Lloyd for evidence of guilt, but his husband was smiling widely. The party was so far, miraculously, a success.

"It's quite a house, quite a house," said Billings, moving closer to Brant, dabbing his wide, sweaty brow. "You're brave fellows."

"Don't start with that mumbo jumbo," Lloyd said. "We need more drinks out here. I should have brought them. It's so hot!"

There were constant high-pitched popping sounds, reminding Brant of the Independence Day bottle rockets of his youth. Yet these in Delhi were launched for something far more spiritual.

"Show me how you mixed that batch of coconut martinis?" said Benny loudly, moving swiftly toward the house, biceps and chest popping through his form-fitting cotton top. John sighed heavily looking increasingly wilted as he followed.

Brant huddled with Billings, Samir and Mendah. Billings repeatedly dabbed his fleshy forehead, smiling in an artificial way.

"I'm a gossip," Billings said, his voice a touch slurred. "I hope you don't mind."

He leaned forward, as if ready to share a terrible secret.

"You know about the scandal, yes?" Billings began.

Brant stepped back, his mind racing with an instinctual mystical knowing, as if the very earth behind him and the bent little tree were drawing him away from what would surely be an ugliness. He wished Jasmine were there.

"There was a British woman that lived here," he began. "In this very house!"

"Oh dear," Mendah said softly, turning to Brant. "Your Carol!"

"Oh yes, I think that was her name. You sneak. You already know. Let me tell it," Billings said shrilly.

His eyes flared and he laced his sweaty, pudgy fingers together as if in prayer.

"It's a horror really. They say it started the turn against the Brits. It was in all the tabloids. I was thrilled to come to this house. *Her* house."

Brant noticed Samir watching him, and saw too a gentle understanding as if the man sensed his growing panic over a ripping open of his secret discovery, his private communing with Carol.

"Billings, you are making our host uncomfortable, it's Diwali after all. A time for unity," Samir said.

Turning quickly towards Samir, Billings laughed very loudly with an edge of harshness.

"Look who's talking! You're no different than me, come on."

From the house, two Indian men emerged carrying large trays of lit candles. Slowly, they began to set them on the lawn near an intricate Diwali floral decoration. It was a large circle, six feet in diameter, bordered with golden marigolds mixed with gerberas and jasmine. Within the circle were hundreds of small orange petals and at the center, an eight-sided star shape.

"Samir is right, tonight is sacred," Mendah said.

"Oh Poo and Fooey," said Billings. "It's a party for Christ's sake! Don't be tiresome. They still write about it. There was an article just a few years ago. That woman is living in Delhi."

"Carol," Brant said a bit too loudly.

"Hell no, the friend Miriam," said Billings, turning away sharply from the trio and heading unsteadily toward the house. "You're all too virtuous for me."

A swarm of guests came out onto the lawn, watching as the two young men moved gingerly, gently, distributing dozens of candles across the wide lawn, creating a soft, mesmerizing glow as, from the distance, the fireworks rang ceaselessly, and people tripped around giddily like children at a summer carnival unaware what any of it really meant.

Chapter 31

The party had dwindled to a half-dozen hangers-on, those dewy late-night drinkers lounging too closely together in chairs or sprawled in messy little groups on the sofa, comforted by an intoxicated intimacy that would disappear before dawn.

The one odd cog in the mix was Billings, whose energy refused to be lulled despite his excessive drinking. He never stopped moving, out to the lawn, watching distant fireworks, singing a duet with the wife of a local salesman and finally insisting the group play charades before they call it quits. It was 3 a.m. Brant was in the kitchen with Lloyd. They stood side by side at the sink. They were washing rose-tinted Baccarat champagne flutes that Mendah had brought as a gift. They were delicate so Brant told the hired help to leave them for him. It was something his mother did after house parties. Her precious china, the crystal tumblers, she washed them by hand. He sighed, handing a flute to Lloyd to dry. He hadn't thought of his mother in a while. She'd been eclipsed by Carol.

"No, it's a book. A book! Don't they play this game in India?"

It was Billings in the living room, cajoling the group to participate. Brand rinsed, then handed another flute.

"He's odd," Brant said softly. "And rude."

Lloyd turned and sleepily kissed Brant on the forehead.

"He manages one of our biggest accounts. Not to be fooled with but," his voice dropped to a whisper. "We have too many glasses."

Brant smiled acknowledging his husband.

"No! This means *sounds like*, Oh Christ," Billings screeched.

He'd never asked Billings about the Carol "scandal". He didn't like or trust the man. Yet he desperately needed closure with Carol's story.

Through the window, he heard classical Indian music – a melody of sounds Brant recognized as Carnatic. It came from a distance. The group was moving from the living room out to the back lawn to investigate.

"Should we?" Brant said.

Lloyd smiled.

"You go, I'll finish up."

Brant left and followed the little troupe. They had scattered drunkenly, plopping into chairs or onto the grass. The music continued. He couldn't determine its source, or how far in the distance it was.

"It's an obsession."

It was Billings.

"That ancient style of music. They devote their lives to perfecting it. It's insane," he said.

He moved closer to Brant, placing a hand on his shoulder to steady himself in the lawn. Brant stiffened, instinctually repulsed by the heavy man's sweaty touch and his snap judgment of a sacred melody. Billings, oblivious, left his hand there, swaying lightly to the music. There was a sudden, loud punctuation of fireworks.

Despite these occasional blasts, the evening was softening. Billings sighed deeply.

"It's all so hopeless," Billings said.

Brant turned to him.

"What is?" Brant said.

Billings turned to him and for a moment Brant sensed the man was going to press back his veil of crass hilarity and share something true.

"Oh hell, I need another drink.," Billings said.

Brant touched his arm, stopping him.

"Can you tell me what happened to the woman that lived here? You never finished your story."

Billings' cheeks flushed a bright red.

"Well all right! But we need to sit down," Billings said.

Billings moved to a small table near the entrance to the house. He collapsed into a patio chair, beckoning his listener. There was something forever unpleasant about the man, Brant thought, unsavory and untrustworthy but at the same time deeply sad. He didn't really want to sit with him, but he felt he had to know. It was Carol, after all. Maybe the truth could save her.

He sat across from Billings. Mendah had led the stragglers to the back garden. They were talking loudly and Mendah's laughter punctuated the night. Brant saw, in the distance, a small flock of green birds approaching. He imagined they were fleeing the fireworks.

"I'm surprised they haven't made her story into a film," Billings began.

From his front shirt pocket, he pulled out a packet of cigarettes, plucked one, lit it and ceremoniously puffed and blew smoke in small circles. He paused, grinning. Relishing the moment, it seemed.

"How do you know the story?" Brant said.

"I was a journalist before I sold my soul to the devil and went corporate," Billings said. "I wrote for *The Sun* in London."

Brant smiled. He'd heard of the paper, one of the trashier tabloids. A potpourri of fact and pulpy fiction. The sound of the approaching birds grew louder, a blend of bold caws and short melodic chirping. He could see them more clearly now. In addition to the pretty green birds, there was a group of larger crow-like birds flying just west. It was as if they were all fleeing at the same time, tired of the noisy festivities. Brant wondered if the larger birds would overtake the smaller bright cluster.

"I interviewed the friend, Miriam, ten years back. A fifty-year anniversary piece. She was a plucky old gal," he said, tossing his head back theatrically, drawing further on the cigarette. "Not bad looking. If you know what I mean. Well preserved in all the right places. I went to her place with a photographer. She was all dolled up in a tweed suit with high heels. Can you imagine?"

Brant bristled at Billing's flippancy. He made everything sound cheap and dirty. He summoned a memory of Miriam, his Miriam, the Miriam of the journal. Elegant and sharp.

Overhead, the green and black birds were crossing paths, simultaneously changing course, though not in a crashing or violent way. Their two tribes seemed to communicate, turning north and south, cutting across the sky, never colliding though flying close.

"Is she still alive?" Brant asked.

"Miriam? Could be. Like I said, she was well preserved."

Mendah wandered over, pulling up a chair, joining their small circle.

"Are we done?" she said.

"Billings is going to tell me about Carol," Brant said.

"Oh!" Mendah said, then with gentleness. "I'm glad."

"Yes," Billings said.

For a moment, he seemed to lose steam, as if the build-up were the thing. Brant wondered if there really was a story to tell.

"The thrust of it all happened at a terrible little hotel near Old Delhi. Carol was the only survivor. Her pretty little white dress covered in blood. That's what got her the front page. *The Sun* took that photo. The Indian police leading her out, the bright American woman. There was real terror in her eyes."

"Hand me a cigarette," Mendah said.

Billings gave her a smoke. Brant looked up at the empty sky. The birds had moved on, the fireworks had stopped. Billings continued.

"She'd gotten tangled up with a bad sort. Ajan Kumar. He wasn't much really, a two-bit pimp and drug dealer. He sold opium, that sort of thing. But he killed a man and copped a plea, which is what got the whole thing rolling with poor Carol. She was his lover of course. He was quite a big thick sort of man, if you like that type. Completely unlike her dull American husband."

It was the second time he'd said Carol's name aloud in the telling, and Brant shivered in the heat, sensing she was listening, her spirit hovering over her old house, ready to swoop down and attack Billings if he veered from the truth.

"When he got arrested, he agreed to work both sides. Like a double agent," Billing said.

"You're making this up," Mendah said. "It's some book you read."

He sat up in his chair, enthusiasm and bravado building.

"Not true! *The Sun* did a big splashy story. You can look it up," he said.

"Let him finish," Brant said, anxious to get it done with.

"The bad guys, you know the drug dealers, they were keen to get back a shit load of drugs. The deal that went wrong for Ajan, it was a delivery and the merchandise went missing after the cops burst in and the smoke cleared. On the outside, it was thought that Ajan knew where the missing drugs were stashed. What they didn't know is he was working with the cops."

Mendah stood up and yawned loudly.

"Holy Christ it's too late for all this, I can't follow you. And I still don't believe a word of it," she said.

"Hey!" Billings said loudly.

Brant turned to Mendah, taking her hand.

"Let's hear the rest. Tell us about Carol."

Billings smiled.

"Oh yes. Ajan told the police Carol was involved. Which Miriam denies flatly. But the cops bought it. They got Carol to believe she was in danger and if she didn't meet up with some very bad people and tell them where the drugs were hidden, the thugs would kill her!"

Brant tried to put the pieces together, based on Carol's

journal, but it was all a jumble.

Billings stood, looking skyward, wobbling a bit as he delivered his finale with cheap grandeur.

"She was a pawn. The police frightened her into believing a bunch of hooey. She agreed to some crazy setup to ensnare the criminals. To get them to turn over a bunch of money for the hidden drugs. Miriam said Carol was mostly afraid of her husband finding out she cheated. Isn't that strange? Drug deals and murder and she was worried about a little infidelity. Oh, the scandal of it all!"

"Is that it?" Mendah said.

Billings laughed, then yawned.

"Oh mostly. The whole setup, her meeting the drug people, the police bursting in, it was a big mess. Somehow, she survived it. Must have dove under a divan when the bullets flew. Though she had all that blood on her dress. That's in the photo. Anyway, she had her fifteen minutes. Scandalized British housewife. Diplomat hubby. Sordid affair, drugs, scandal. It sold a few papers."

At that, he took a short bow and turned to go. Brant called out.

"Wait," he said. "What about Miriam?"

He did not turn, kept walking, spent and finally done, his voice fading as he moved away.

"Oh, she might still be around. I've got her address in my files if you want to go and gawk. She's…"

One last burst of fireworks rang out as a fiery dawn made itself felt and Billings vanished into the house.

Chapter 32

Brant hailed a tuk tuk bound for the East Patel Nagar neighborhood of Delhi. He settled into the straw seat for a bumpy ride. It was early evening. Billings had given him an address for Miriam, though jostling along the road through a maze of traffic in the heat, dust spraying, he had his doubts whether he would find her. Billings, Lloyd said, was known for mixing fact with fiction.

After a lengthy trip across a highway and through a weave of streets crowded with stray dogs and children, he was deposited in the center of a very narrow stone road lined with stout, whitewashed buildings, with some balconies and others anchored by dirty, hackneyed signs advertising food and clothing. At the end of the road was the entrance to a park. A statue towered.

The driver waved toward an alley, indicating the address, but Brant first walked toward the statue, knowing what it was, both thrilled and frightened. He knew some end was coming.

It was a twenty-foot rendition of Hanuman, the Hindu monkey god. This version in red clay was immediately arousing for Brant, more man than animal, rising toward the sky on strong legs, a broad muscular chest, its head topped with the traditional crown. He recalled how uneasy he felt when he saw Hanuman in Cold Spring. And he realized now at last, standing, cowering at its mighty feet, that his Cold Spring infidelity, that reckless and selfish moment that preceded his adventure to Delhi, had not been a summoned, mystical thing, had not been a dizzying lapse: it had been a lusty, hard and determined pressing down of a rooted grief that would not be silenced, that shattering and irreconcilable loss of his mother.

He turned away from the smirking beast, and sat now at the base of the statue, watching the frenetic, constant movement of the street ahead. He drew in a deep breath lowered his head and heard for just a moment his mother's voice, that distinct laughter that came with the telling of a story and then immediately beyond that a sense that her memory was too rapidly moving away. Facing the ever-deafening noise of Delhi he raised his head and cut loose with a long, ragged cry wailing shamelessly until he had no breath left, until he had to slump over in defeat. Then he got up to go find Miriam.

Chapter 33

Her flat was in a narrow alleyway, next to a café that sold coffee and adjacent to a strange little storefront featuring a water-soaked wooden sign that simply said "Theater." Miriam's building was three stories, with small, rusted iron balconies.

At the building entrance, Brant considered what he would say to her. She lived on the top floor. He paused, trying to think of a phrase, question or plea but nothing came. He rang the bell. The door buzzed open. No one asked who he was.

The staircase was one of those divided into two segments of six steps with a turn and a landing between flights. It felt like a hike, and he wondered how a woman her age could manage it. He knew she had to be over eighty. Again, he thought it might be a ruse, a Billings creation.

At the top, he caught his breath. He heard chanting music coming from 3C, her flat. It was at the end of the landing. He moved cautiously, listening for voices. If he heard young people cavorting, he would dash away. At the door he paused. There was nothing but the sound of the chant. He knocked. Nothing. He knocked again and through the wooden door came a strangled cry as if someone were gasping for air, making a herculean effort to be heard. There was another sound. Something knocking against the floor, and then a woman's voice.

"Use your key," she cried.

Brant froze, glancing down the dimly lit hallway. Tentatively, he knocked once more.

"What the hell is wrong with you," the voice said weakly but with emphasis.

The door opened. An elderly, white-haired woman with a spray of lilac in her swept-up bun and a silk knee-length purple dress with a rounded low collar stared at him. Her skin was very pale, powdered lightly with a circle of rouge at each cheek. She balanced on a gold tipped cane.

"Who in the hell are you?" she said.

Before he could speak, there was the thumping of heavy footsteps climbing the stairs. The white-haired woman took a deep breath trying to raise her weak, rattling voice to be heard.

"Falak, hurry up! There's a strange man here."

The footsteps continued and Brant backed away. He'd already made a mess of this. Turning, he saw a sturdy heavy-set Indian woman in a floral housecoat, wearing thick black glasses and carrying a tote bag. She came quickly toward him.

"Get away from there," the woman yelled.

Brant could not escape without running over the woman in the narrow hallway.

"I'm looking for Miriam," he said weakly. "I found this."

From his satchel, he pulled out the weathered journal. Falak pushed past him, into the apartment.

"Did he hurt you?" she said to the old woman.

The white-haired woman stood very still, balancing on her cane. She brought her free hand to her chin, rubbing it for a moment. She looked at the journal he held.

"Miriam is dead," she said. "Come in."

Chapter 34

They sat across from one other in the main room of the apartment, positioned on matching settees, both seats covered in rich floral patterns featuring hibiscus and dahlias. There were also birds, long-necked yellow birds, floating across the seats' silk fabric. Falak had gotten them settled, then darted off down a hallway. She was making a ruckus in the kitchen.

The older woman held the journal, which Brant had given to her. She wore bedroom slippers that matched the purple of her silk dress, and a thin strand of pearls. He guessed she was just past eighty. She was very frail looking, but the whisper of a younger feminine attractiveness lingered like a shadow.

"Are you here to blackmail me?" she said with a wry smile.

There was a low, wooden coffee table between them with a small golden box on top of it, this too emblazoned with the image of a yellow bird. She slowly, and with great care, leaned her old body toward the box, took out a cigarette and put it in her hand before straightening back up. She did not light it.

"I read the journal, so I thought..."

Brant paused. His thoughts were jumbled again.

"I was told Miriam lived here," he said.

Falak bustled in with a tray which she deposited onto

the table. Then she looked at the old woman, pulled a lighter from her housecoat, lit the cigarette, and went back toward the kitchen.

"Would you be kind enough to pour. No ice," the old woman said.

On the tray was a bottle of Rye, two glasses and a beautifully polished ice bucket. He poured the drinks.

"Miriam was such a tattletale," the woman said, drawing on the cigarette. "But then she needed the money."

Falak reappeared and spoke in a very loud voice.

"Why are you here?" she said to Brant accusingly, wagging a finger at him.

The older woman turned to her sharply.

"Falak, shame on you. We haven't had a visitor in months. Who really cares what brought him? He brought this," she said, lifting the journal.

She turned to Brant as he poured Rye into a glass.

"I forgot all about it, that was so long ago," she said. "I of course am Carol."

The announcement startled him, and he dumped too much liquor into the glass, slopping it onto the table. Carol did not seem to notice. He took in a breath, wondering what was wrong with him, how he had failed to put it all together when he walked in. He looked up at her, a thrill of joy and a rush of emotions, as if something dead had come to life, and then too, he thought of his mother. Her shadow hovering.

"We shared this place, it was Miriam's first," Carol said. "So, what do you want to know from an old bird like me?"

She slowly lifted the glass to her lips, sipping, then began to cross her legs, that shadow of youth again, but thought better of what seemed to be a great effort and sat still. Brant took a drink. Then took another. It felt unreal. But then so did so many things in Delhi.

"I live at your house. I found that buried under a tree," he said as if this were a sane explanation as to why he had come. "What happened? The story didn't end."

"Oh yes," Carol said. "Are you a reporter?"

Falak, who had been lingering, took a seat on a mahogany chair with a woven straw back.

"No," Brant said. "I'm nothing really."

The idea struck him as true, though he'd never identified himself in such a way. But here, with this strange figure come to life from a series of inked sentences and long-ago musings, he knew he had no real purpose in Delhi, not like Lloyd or even Mendah. He was simply a lingering thing, looking for meaning in Carol. Needing her to give him direction.

"Oh, I get that," Carol said. "I can tell you the end if you'd like."

"Very much," he said.

"Falak, bring us something sweet." Then to Brant as Falka got up and disappeared, "I don't like to eat much anymore. It comes with age. Some whiskey and sweets. That's all."

She leaned forward and put out her cigarette, took another short drink, then sat heavily against the back of the settee. Brant admired the slow, deliberate elegance of her movements, which he imagined was due to the pain of old bones, but it was lovely to watch none the less.

"I broke my husband's heart, that's the end really. But

you want all of it I suppose."

Falak returned with a plate of small powdery cookies. She set them down then retook her chair. Carol took up a cookie, bit it.

"Oh, I love these," she said. "Take one please. What exactly do you want to know? I'm getting tired."

Brant took a cookie but did not bite into it, only held it in his hand which was now spotted white with the loose dust of powdered sugar. He felt a new urgency, as if she would demand he leave any minute. He thought of his mother, that train trip, those scones. He brushed that away. He had to focus.

"You were going to see a dangerous man. Ajan your lover was in prison," Brant said with a new fervor.

"Oh, I don't want to tell that part," Carol said, biting the white cookie again and finishing it.

"Go on!" Falka said loudly, smiling for the first time since he'd walked in.

"Oh, that's not the best of it. Not the heart. But yes they were very bad men. Ajan had painted me as some sort of harlot who was in on it all, which maybe I was."

"The police are dirty men," Falka said, standing and taking two cookies for herself, one which she deposited into her housecoat pocket.

At that Carol laughed lightly, then yawned slowly, elaborately.

"What went wrong?" Brant said, trying to contain his growing enthusiasm.

Carol glanced at him, as if discovering him there for the first time. It seemed to take her a moment to register the question and regain where they had been.

"A man was shot. Ajan had some deal with the police to finger the bad men. It all went so wrong. But that's not the point, you must see that."

For a moment she became animated, sitting forward, her eyes flaring, as if she were explaining a sacred riddle.

"What is the point?" Brant said, confused, but not wanting to slow her down.

"Well, if you can't see it."

She shut her eyes and yawned deeply.

"All right enough," Falka said, standing at attention and staring intently at Brant, the interloper.

"What is the point?" he said once more, with emphasis.

Carol opened her eyes and looked directly at him, sighing.

"My husband left me. Dropped me immediately. Once he knew I cheated. It was that - that he could not forgive. It ruined us. That was my tragedy."

"His loss. Asshole," said Falak. "Now we are done. Get out, Mister."

Brant kept his eyes on Carol, ignoring Falak who was moving closer to him.

"I did that too," Brant said.

"Did what?" Falak said.

Eyes on Carol, he continued.

"I cheated on my husband. But he didn't leave."

At this Carol perked up once more and Falak halted.

"Really!" Carol said. "He stayed?"

Brant did not hesitate.

"I fell apart. I think he saw how desperately I really love

128

him."

"And he you, dear, if he stayed." Carol said. "So, your story is nothing like mine. Thank God."

At that, she lifted both her hands in the air and Brant moved closer thinking she was reaching for him and they would touch, but Falak took her hands and helped her up, then began to guide her out of the main room, down the hall.

He watched her ancient back in the elegant silk dress drift away, the very slow movements of each leg, one then another, step by step, guided by Falak and for a moment, he saw himself as her, Lloyd at his side, the two walking toward something which was framed by light, not darkness as he so often imagined, only a bright and warming light, a certain foreverness.

www.ingramcontent.com/pod-product-compliance
Lightning Source LLC
Chambersburg PA
CBHW060354180626
46817CB00008B/3002